Panda-monium Within Me

PANDA-MONIUM WITHIN ME

MONIQUE RUSS

Playlist

Available on Spotify

"Time in a Tree" – Raleigh Ritchie

"C7osure (You Like)" – Lil Nas X

"Enough" – Hippie Sabotage

"Rule the World" – Michael Kiwanuka

"All Day" – E-40 ft. Gucci Mane

"Feel." – Kendrick Lamar

"New Magic Wand" – Tyler, The Creator

"I'm Not Okay, But I Know I'm Going to Be" – Raleigh Ritchie

"Always Forever" – Cults

"Got it on Me" – Pop Smoke

"Grave of Broken Dreams" – Mat Bastard

"Panda" – Desiigner

"Bad Habit" – Steve Lacey

"Reborn" – Kids See Ghosts

"Turtle in the Waves" – Hippie Sabotage

To your inner voice: I see you and you are not alone

Author's Note

Panda-monium Within Me contains mature content that is not suitable for all readers. Please be mindful of your mental health. Reader discretion is advised.

Content Warnings: child abuse (historical, non-graphic), sexual harassment (non-graphic), bullying, death of a parent, drugs, self-harm (historical), gun violence, and mental health.

CHAPTER ONE

Drew rolled over onto his back at the sound of his radio suddenly blaring today's hits. He stared up at the popcorn ceiling. Exhaustion was already starting to claw at him. He was up late last night, again. Drew was not looking forward to starting another day. At least today was Friday. The bubbly, nauseating pop song bled into his room. It seemed to grow louder the longer he stared up into the abyss. Footsteps from the floor above quietly drummed into his room.

"You're going to be late if you don't get up." Drew's familiar inner voice nagged at him. *"Evie is probably already up. Mom is probably already gone,"* the voice continued to scold. The little black cloud he woke up with seemed to grow bigger. Drew sighed, summoning the strength to remove himself from his warm, comforting bed. He staggered over to his bathroom

thankful that his whole room was the basement where he was free to wander around in his boxers and let his skin feel the cool air until he had to cover it.

He stared at his mediocre, caramel colored body as he lazily brushed his teeth. Disgust began to fill him as he stared at the scars all over his midsection. The year he spent cutting himself filled him with disappointment. "*You're ugly*," his little voice whispered. "*You're weak. How does this help any-one?*" His handiwork was all over the place. A few scars here and there on his calves and thighs. A few on his hips. He counted them. He counted them every morning, "*17.*"

Seventeen jaded, misdirected markings into his light brown skin marred his body like nicks in a tree.

Three scars on his right hip, toward his belly button. Four cuts on his inner left thigh. Five on the outside of his right thigh. Three on his left calf. And two on his right calf.

His stomach flipped violently with repulsion. Drew wished he hadn't done this to himself when he had turned thirteen. Somehow, he thought it would help. When one cut wasn't enough, he made another cut. Then another. All year he'd allowed the vile voice to drive him to cut himself. Now it only served as a hideous reminder. Drew hadn't worn shorts in four years. He was seventeen now. And he still felt like the oppressed kid he was all those summers ago.

"*What would Mom think? What would Evie think?*" The voice continued.

Drew felt the inner voice gain more power as his mind worked.

He continued to stare at his scars and tried to let his mind go blank, brushing his teeth on autopilot. Drew wasn't able to silence his thoughts for long. He thought about everything he had to do for the day. He needed to take Evie to school and catch up on yesterday's homework. Drew couldn't remember if there was a quiz in his History class. He'd have to find a way to make it up since it was first period.

"*There's not enough time in the day!*" The voice became louder.

Drew groaned and rolled his eyes. Spitting into the sink, he continued with his morning routine. Suddenly, another being poofed into existence next to Drew. Drew had made it a whole ten minutes by himself before he had willed Panda into existence.

"*Good morning!*" Panda purred.

Panda was essentially human. He had a human body and was very tall and lanky like Drew. His skin was midnight black. The only thing that clued Drew into knowing Panda was a figment of his wild imagination was the fact that Panda had the head of a Panda Bear. This was strange to Drew because his imaginary friend could still emote and had facial expressions like a human. Drew supposed if he made a practical Panda mask with latex and movie magic, this is what it would be. Panda nearly looked cute. But Drew knew better. This was no imaginary friend to him. Panda was his worst nightmare incarnate.

All his insecurities, impulsive control issues, anger, fear, anything Drew thought was negative about himself was all wrapped up in soft fur, round ears, and black eyes.

"*Oh, come on!*" Panda scoffed at the belittlement. "*That's not all I do. I'm also your biggest fan!*" Drew hated to admit it. But Panda had his supportive moments. They were just so few and far between that Drew never noticed them.

Drew didn't get two words in before Panda started rambling, "*Do you think Mom's at work?*" Panda pressed his face into the mirror and fussed over his fur. "*Liam is probably awake. Freaking jerk. I can't remember if we finished the biology homework. What's the point? We've only got a few weeks left before summer and I'm not so confident you...*"

Drew tuned Panda out at that point. His ramblings were all over the place. Every fifth word or so drifted through

Drew's consciousness, but only stayed for half a second until the next concern passed through. It was like trying to fixate on one tree while staring out the window of a speeding car. Even if Drew wanted to keep up with the racing unfiltered thoughts, he couldn't do much about it.

"*Why are you ignoring me this morning?!*" Panda yelled in Drew's ear.

Drew flinched slightly, not expecting the sudden noise or Panda's fur to tickle his ear. Drew finished washing his face and put some deodorant on. He reached for his coarse brush and roughly brushed down on his tight, black curls.

"I'm not ignoring you," Drew lied.

"*Yes, you are!*" Panda accused. "*You haven't even looked at me or said anything.*"

"I'm getting ready, dude." Drew grumbled.

"*Fine,*" Panda harrumphed. "*So long as you promise you're not mad at me. Now, order of business! Biology homework.*"

Drew looked at his exposed skin one more time. His eyes lingered on the imperfections on his hip bone and his too long legs before he turned around and violently flicked off the bathroom light. He picked up various articles of clothing, first smelling them to see if they were clean or dirty, and then proceeded to drop them back on the floor as he passed.

"It's only half done. I'll have to work on it in English."

"*But that's how we'll get behind in English,*" Panda criticized. "*Let's work on biology homework during lunch. You know something? I've always wanted to try biting off a finger. I've heard it takes the same amount of force as biting off a carrot. We have to go check on Evie. Hurry up!*" Panda groaned as he dressed in the clothes Drew disregarded. "*I hate the weekends. Work and keeping Evie occupied. Mom's probably working…*"

Drew, now dressed in a t-shirt and black jeans, packed up his bag and headed upstairs. Panda was right on his heels. He was still rambling on about random useless facts and showering Drew with rapid thoughts he had.

"*Did you know Australia is wider than the moon?! I wonder what movie is at the theaters. Maybe we could take Evie! But shit, this weekend is probably the best time to prep for finals. You're definitely going to fail math.*"

With each step up the stairs, Drew's feet felt heavier and heavier. His chest constricted. He didn't know who was upstairs already. In anticipation of the worse, he threw his guard up.

CHAPTER TWO

"Drew!"

For the first time, and probably for the last time of the day, Drew genuinely smiled, momentarily weakening his shield. His little sister, Evie, was beaming at him over her cereal bowl. He half waved at her. His momentum carried him to the kitchen. Drew's happiness burned out as quickly as it flared when he spotted Liam sitting at the table beside her.

"Morning', dude. You look rough. Sleep ok?" Liam asked over his coffee cup.

Drew ignored his question and entered the kitchen, leaving Panda to make crude gestures and scream absurd insults inches from Liam's face. It was hard to take him seriously since he was skinnier than Drew. But Liam didn't notice. No one ever noticed Panda. Only Drew. Imaginary friend rules and all.

"Are you almost ready for school, Evie?" Drew dropped some Pop-Tarts in the toaster. He turned toward the fridge. His heart sank as he saw the sticky note his mom left behind. This morning. Last night. Who knew?

STICKY NOTE: I'm working a double. Liam will be home today.

Evie shook her head with eagerness. "My teeth and my hair is left. Can you do it? Please, Drew."

"Of course!" Panda answered for him. Since Panda had some control over Drew's emotions, sometimes things would get blurted out without Drew's permission. Drew worked hard to hide Panda. Panda could never be seen, maybe sometimes heard, but never seen.

Drew turned back to his sister at the table. He peered over the kitchen counter to look at her and ignored the dark presence sitting next to her. He forced a small smile. "And then we've got to head out."

Liam turned the corner of his mouth down as he shrugged. "I was going to take her to school this morning."

Drew dropped his fake smile and turned to the man Panda was sticking his tongue out at. "I'll take her."

Liam choked on a condescending snort. He grabbed his mug and headed toward the sink. Drew's stomach dropped. He shrank against the counter by the toaster, wishing for the little machine to hurry up and release his breakfast.

"You'll miss first period."

Liam's dark presence threatened to consume him. Drew crossed his arms in defiance. As if the stance was a reinforced shield. Liam's coffee breath caused Drew's stomach to churn. "Then I miss first period."

Liam shook his head in mock concern. He dumped the remainder of his coffee in the sink. "I'm not sure how your mother would feel about that."

He looked Drew up and down. Drew leaned back against the counter even more, trying to create more distance in the small kitchen. He grew uneasy under Liam's green scrutinizing eyes that slowly raised up to his panicked brown eyes. Drew hated green.

"You know, it's supposed to be really nice today. Like high of sixty?" Liam attempted to be friendly again.

"Why do you care about what I wear?" Drew let Panda's jeering question pass his lips before he could stop it. Acting like an alpha, silver-back gorilla, Panda thumped his chest in domination of Liam.

Liam shook his head and returned to the dining room table. "Have a great day at school, kiddo."

Liam bent down and kissed Evie on the cheek. The simple action caused Evie to kick her legs more in appreciation. Drew's spine went stiff in apprehension. Panda started to see red. Liam threw a smirk at Drew and then headed down the hall toward his room. Drew stared at his back. When the door softly closed, Drew turned his attention to his sister. Her wide, amber eyes were watching him carefully.

"Why don't you like Uncle Liam?" the heavy metal spoon weighed down her small hand. It slightly clinked against her bowl.

"*Shit!*" Panda began pacing frantically around the room. "*She is so smart. Do you think she knows? No! Of course, she doesn't know. No one knows. But she knows something is up. We have to do a better job. But she's right! We don't like Uncle Liam. But we can't tell her why! But we can't lie to her. Well, I can. You're shit at lying. Look at that sweet face! But she can't know!*"

Panda began to spiral.

Drew sucked on his teeth and tried to ignore Panda as he panicked and paced around the room in a tight circle. Drew's face twisted as he picked his words. "We just don't get along right now."

Evie looked down at her now empty bowl in thought. Her round face started to turn sad.

"You done?" Drew slightly cocked his head. He looked for a subject change. Some way to move this morning along and distance themselves from Uncle Liam. Evie smiled at him proudly. "Put your bowl in water and let's go do your hair really quick."

Evie hurriedly put her bowl in the sink and ran to the bathroom. With help from her big brother, she jumped up on the counter and sat looking toward the mirror, her face sandwiched between Drew's and Panda's cheeks. Drew ran the faucet, waiting for the water to get warm.

"It's Friday," Drew declared. "What's our Friday-do?"

Panda quietly chanted, "*Please no Elsa. Please no Elsa. Please no Elsa. You seriously need to practice how to do that stupid braid, bro. Last time, it didn't look the greatest. We can't let our sister look like a hot mess.*"

"Bunnies!" Evie answered.

Seeing her gap-toothed grin, Drew's guard dropped a little and a smile leaked out.

"Good choice!" Panda exclaimed for Evie to hear.

"Up or down?" Drew asked.

"I want...I want..." She brought her hands up to her

head, trying to explain the design. "I want…" Evie licked her lips. "…up bunnies, like Princess Leia."

"*Yeah, that sounds great!*" Panda beamed.

"I'll do my best," Drew quickly followed up, attempting to curb Panda's excitement.

Suppressing a chuckle, he hurriedly got to work. Putting warm water in a spray bottle, he sprayed her tangled, chocolate curls. She covered her face with a towel. She always hated that part. He spritzed some leave-in conditioner a few times and then dabbed at her hair with the hand towel, collecting loose water. Gently, he parted her hair down the middle. Combing out each side, he gathered her hair into two high ponytails. Evie watched him in the mirror as he concentrated solely on her tresses.

Panda tried to talk to her, of course, interjecting some of his random concerns about the day in the middle. Evie didn't hear him. She was focused on the way her big brother's thick brows met in the middle as he wove her hair into two braids. He quickly wrapped her hair at the base. With another twist, he tied the bundle off. He hugged her from behind and kissed her cheek. She squealed in delight as she hopped off the counter and grabbed her toothbrush.

Drew strolled to the living room to find their backpacks

and checked her bag. He pulled out her agenda and found a pen. He initialed by yesterday's date for her. Normally it was the parent's job to sign off on the agenda. But he doubted Liam knew about this responsibility, and his mom's random schedule made the task unreliable. Drew didn't have a problem doing it. He felt responsible to make sure she got to and from school. He made sure her homework was done and helped her with school projects. What was one daily initial compared to all that?

Satisfied that she had her reading book, school ID, and homework in her bag, he returned her agenda and zipped it closed. She bounced into the living room, excited at the prospect of her Friday now that she had a good hair day. He put her backpack on her, and asked if she was ready to go.

Drew and Panda ignored the shrine to their father in the corner of the living room as Evie waved goodbye to his picture. A whole corner curio devoted to a ghost who was dedicated to haunting Drew. Faint memories turned into false judgement. *"Nope! Not today. Shove it down,"* Panda ordered him. Drew gently pushed his sister out on the front step and locked the door behind them, not bothering to let their uncle know they were leaving. Drew's cold Pop-Tarts stayed put, forgotten in the toaster.

Panda and Drew held Evie's hands as they walked her to school. It was about a twenty-minute detour from his school by foot and worth the trouble if it meant Liam didn't take her to school. Drew and Panda listened intently to Evie as she retold a dream she had last night. "And then, Mr. Sprinkles ate the whole cake! I thought it was funny, but he felt bad."

When they got to Evie's school, they had a group hug. "Alright," Drew grabbed her shoulders, "I'll be here after school to get you." Like he always was.

For the past year, Drew had missed his first period History class to take her to school, and last semester he ditched his seventh period to walk her back home. Thankfully, he had seventh period off this semester. One less class to make up. Evie held her pinkie out to him.

With a half-attempted smile, he grabbed her pinkie with his, and straightened up a bit to hit the inside of his ankle with her ankle. Evie burst into laughter at Drew's dorky pose.

"Promise," Panda said. And Evie heard.

With the blaring school bell announcing it was time to find homeroom, Evie gave Drew a wave before darting into the school. Her sparkly backpack bounced wildly against her back. Drew and Panda waited until she was inside the school before they made their way to the high school.

CHAPTER THREE

At lunch, Drew copied the History class notes he missed that morning from Wynter. Panda sat beside him, shoving French Fries into his mouth.

Wynter wrapped her fingers around her Diet Coke can. Her painted black nails drummed against the metal in slow rhythm. Her wild, black curls shook slightly as she disagreed with something. Trey chuckled at something she said. His wide frame shook slightly, causing the table's surface to tremble. The conversation between Drew's two best friends was muffled.

Drew swallowed hard, trying to dislodge the lump that was quickly forming. Panda noticed. *"We should engage now,"* Panda pestered. *"Are you done with those notes? It's not like you're going to study anyways. They're leaving you in the dust!"*

"Drew?" Wynter repeated.

To Panda's relief Drew finally looked up. His hand was thankful for the break. "Sorry, what?"

"Did you hear me?" Wynter's soft grey eyes widened in expectation. Her dark skin seemed flawless. Panda caused butterflies in Drew's stomach as he stared too long at his best friend.

"Uh, no," Drew rubbed at the back of his neck. His eyes quickly darted to Trey for respite.

She leaned forward, "Are you going to Prom?" Drew's face twisted in disapproval. She laughed at his response. "Oh, come on! We can all go together as friends!"

"Pfft," Drew sat up. "Can't we go next year? When we're seniors?"

"Wynter's freaking out she won't be here next year," Trey teased.

Drew turned uneasy eyes toward her. He tried to mask it with a smirk. "Have you heard back yet?" Panda drummed the pencil on the table rapidly.

Wynter's eyes fell to the thumping pencil, shaking her head, "I'll know next week."

"Why did she have to sign up for that stupid French transfer program?!" Panda ran his hands down his furry face in anguish.

"Is it all year?" Trey spoke around his food.

"Minimum of a semester. But if I choose to stay the full year, then I'll be back here just in time for graduation."

"*A whole semester…*"

"All the more reason to go to prom this year!" Wynter proclaimed.

"I think we've got time." Drew looked down at his notes.

"Nah dude, watch her fall in love with a French artist," Trey teased.

"Ah madam-muah-selle," Panda clutched at his heart, "falling een luv een zee citee ov luv." Drew continued to mock in a terrible French accent. Trey joined in with his own inaccurate drawl. Wynter insulted them in immaculate French. Which just caused the boys to roll more in laughter.

"You're stuck with us for life!" Trey draped his arm around her shoulder and brought her in close. "We're not going anywhere, Wyn."

"*Well…*WE'RE *not going anywhere. But* SHE *is…She's destined for big, grand things. You're destined to be a loser…*" Panda murmured.

But Wynter was done playing. She pushed Trey's arm off. Her smile dropped as she locked eyes with Drew, scared she and Trey had caused a trigger for him. Trey read her face immediately and looked at his friend across the table.

"Sorry dude," Trey hushed, "I didn't mean…"

"It's fine," Panda brushed it off. Honestly, Drew didn't even think of his dad until now. *"And we're not going to!"* Panda continued to dismiss.

"When's prom?" Drew attempted to redirect the conversation. He swatted away Panda's hand and picked at the food left on his tray.

"At the end of the month," Wynter pursed her lips. "Can you believe it's already May?"

"We cappin' off Junior year with a legendary Trey party?" Drew brushed the crumbs off his hands.

"Depends," Trey shrugged. "You bringing' anything?" Trey held his hand up for a high five. Panda returned the gesture with a loud smack that reverberated into the busy cafeteria.

Wynter stared at Drew with disappointment. Disapproval dripped off her tongue. "I thought you were done with that. For Evie?"

"It is for Evie!" Panda exclaimed defensively. "And it's easy money," Drew spoke softer this time.

"Then get a legit job!" Wynter argued.

Drew and Panda stared at her with annoyance. *"She'll*

never understand."

Trey looked back and forth between his quarreling friends.

"Jesus you two!" Trey forced a laugh. "It's always the same old fight with you two."

Wynter slapped him on the arm swiftly, stood up, and grabbed her bag.

"Really?" Panda groaned in agitation.

"I'm heading to the library. Catch you guys later." Wynter looked at Drew for half a second longer before she stormed off.

"What's her problem?"

"Ahh," Trey grabbed the back of his neck, cringing at his friend's behavior. "She just cares a bit too much. You know that." Trey looked like he wanted to say more but decided against it. Instead, he shook his head.

Drew hummed to himself in thought. "You wanna hang out later? After school?" He popped a fry in his mouth.

"Nah, I promised Syd I'd hang out with her tonight. Maybe tomorrow?"

"*Sydney Porter,*" Panda gagged. "*A cheerleader and a jock dating. How cliché.*" Drew agreed with Panda on that one. Sydney was just about the most snobbish girl in the whole school. Well, her whole clique was just about the worst. She didn't approve at all of Drew and Wynter. His chest ached thinking he could've been a football meathead right alongside his best friend, but Drew quit playing football after the season ended when he turned thirteen.

"Shove it down." Panda cautioned.

Drew was really good. He'd been a defensive cornerback. Trey was an outside linebacker and stayed in that position throughout high school. That's how Drew and Trey met, playing little league in fourth grade. Drew could be looking at a scholarship if he had stuck with it. It confused the hell out of his parents when he didn't want to play anymore.

"What did I just say? SHOVE. IT. DOWN!" Panda was losing his patience now.

Drew ignored Panda as he continued to let his mind spiral. Drew quit a lot of things when he was thirteen. Not just football. At the time, people really showed who they were when he withdrew. The year he was cutting himself, he went from the loud, cheerful, class clown to the melancholy kid in black who sat quietly in the back. People he thought were his friends disappeared faster than Evie's Halloween candy. But Trey didn't quit on him. He was grateful for his friend's loyalty. He somehow found Wynter in the middle of his despair. And he'd been grateful for her since.

Panda snapped the pencil in half, overwhelmed by the onslaught of memories. Trey winced at Drew's sudden violence.

"You ok, dude?" Trey's eyebrows pinched with concern.

Drew sighed at the loss of his pencil, shoving it into his backpack. "Yeah," he cleared his throat.

"I should be free tomorrow," Trey offered again, in the hopes to lighten the mood.

"Yeah, no," Drew shook his head, struggling to find his own voice, "don't stress about it."

"UGH! Trey's going to be with his girlfriend tonight. Albeit the worst girl on the planet. But a girlfriend nonetheless. We're going to die ALONE! Who'd want to be with such a screwed-up loser?" Drew forced a small smile while Panda criticized Trey and Sydney in his ear. Attempting to hide his inner turmoil, Drew cleared his throat, barely enough to silence Panda. "Just hit me up, dude."

For the rest of lunch, Panda pulled Drew more inward and kept him focused on copying Wynter's notes. Drew didn't absorb any of the material. His mind was full of his petty resentment of Trey and his annoyance at Wynter's judgement.

CHAPTER FOUR

At the end of lunch, Trey and Drew walked together to Econ class. Drew was thankful to have one class with Trey. He technically had History class with Wynter, but he always missed it. Drew sat in his spot in the back and Trey sat in the desk in front of him. Drew got an extra minute of one-on-one time with his friend before Sydney Porter took up her spot in the desk beside Trey. In true Sydney fashion, she ignored Drew. A few of the other athletes Trey knew also sat around them.

"*See,*" Panda condemned, "*left in the dust! Trey doesn't need you. He has his own friends.*" Drew sat back and watched his friend get swallowed up in the popularity bubble. He placed an earbud in his right ear and half listened to the teacher as the lesson began. And for thirty minutes, Drew enjoyed the silence in his head as Panda disappeared.

The classroom buzzed with chatter toward the end of class as Mrs. Mallard announced the project they would be doing instead of a final. "Trey…" Drew spoke for the first time all period, ready to ask him if he wanted to be partners.

"Trey!" Sydney sang out, interrupting Drew. "Let's be partners."

Trey looked back and forth between his best friend and his girlfriend. Sydney batted her heavy made-up eyes. Trey looked back at Drew and gave him an apologetic look. Feigning patience and understanding, Drew leaned back in his chair. Sydney threw Drew a smug look before Trey saw, and Drew's face screwed up in frustration. And with that Panda popped up again, making snide comments about Sydney.

Drew was only in Panda's negative self-talking bubble for half a second before a tap on his right arm jolted him. He yanked his ear bud out and turned to the source of the touch.

"I'm sorry," a girl to his right he hadn't noticed shrank back.

Drew's eyes widened like Panda's.

She brushed back her chocolate waves behind her ear. Her dark irises blinked back at him with shyness. Her pale cheeks slightly blushed. Drew's throat constricted.

"I'll be your partner if you want," she shrugged.

"Oh, uh…" Drew stammered as Panda frantically hit his arm in stunned disbelief. "*Say something you loser!*" Panda yelled for action.

"Mrs. Mallard said partners were optional," she rambled out. "But Sydney is paired with Trey, and I was wondering if you wanted to work on it together."

"*Miranda Goodman is talking to us!*" Panda continued poking at Drew.

Miranda was part of the cheerleader clique, but Drew couldn't fathom why. She was so much sweeter and quieter than the rest of the group. Drew remembered her fondly in middle school. She was a bookworm with braces and the widest smile on the rare occasion he got to see it. The summer before ninth grade her braces came off and her chest grew a cup size. Her glow-up must have caught the attention of Sydney Porter. Now, under Sydney's vigilant guidance, Miranda wore tighter clothes and perfect makeup. The two were practically attached at the hip.

Miranda normally sat in the seat in front of Sydney, out of Drew's sight. But today, she was suddenly sitting next to him, looking expectant. He glanced around the rest of the room at everyone moving to be closer to their partner. Small groups formed around him. *"Are we the only one without a partner?!"* Panda shrieked in panic.

She let out a breathy laugh that caused Drew's heart to momentarily stop. "I guess a project is preferable to a final."

"Yeah," Drew released a surprised chuckle, finally finding his voice.

He brought his hands down and aggressively wiped off the beads of sweat on his pants. Panda desperately batted at his arm with volatile impatience.

"So, uh…" Miranda fidgeted with her hands and offered a forced smile. "Did you…" she started again.

"Yeah, we can be partners!" Panda blurted out with a little too much enthusiasm for Drew's liking. He was impatient that Drew's own voice had failed him.

Miranda's lukewarm smile changed into a wide grin. She bobbed her head enthusiastically. Her wavy hair pooled over her shoulders at the movement. Drew sucked in a breath.

"We can get started tomorrow if you want?"

"Oh, I, uh," he rubbed the back of his neck, "I've got to watch my sister during the day."

"I have a little sister, too." Miranda placed a surprised hand on her chest.

Before Drew could respond, Trey spun around, injecting

himself in their conversation. "Evie would love Maddison."

Drew squinted at his friend. When would he have met Miranda's sister? "*Through Sydney, duh!*" Panda nearly whacked Drew upside the head.

"Yeah, you should bring her!" Miranda gave a surprised laugh. "They can have a play date while we work."

Drew turned his pinched face to her. This wasn't how he'd planned to spend his weekend. "*We don't know if Mom's working,*" Panda reminded him. "*Liam will probably be home all weekend.*" Drew shuddered at the thought.

Seeing Drew's apprehension, Trey continued, "They're like the same age, I think."

Miranda shrugged, not knowing how old Evie was. "My sister is eight. She's got an insane number of toys. I'm sure they'll get along."

"*Think about it,*" Panda encouraged. "*What was the plan for the weekend? Stay in with Evie? Walk down to the strip and get her an ice cream? She could have a chance to spend time with someone her age.*"

Drew pressed his lips into a tight smile. "Sure, that sounds great."

"Here, give me your phone."

He numbly obeyed her polite command. Miranda

entered her number. Trey winked at him before turning around. Drew caught Sydney's scowl of disapproval. "Text me and I'll give you my address," Miranda instructed, giving him back his phone.

The bell rang rudely. "*No!*" Panda screeched. "*I want to keep talking to her!*" Panda dramatically swooned at the slight brushing of their fingers as she handed him back his phone.

He overhead Sydney say, "It's a miracle he's not a drop-out. You're going to wind up doing that whole project by yourself." Drew put his guard back up. Panda began ranting as they shuffled into the hallway. "*Why is Sydney like this? What did we ever do to her?! We are so going to prove her wrong!*"

Drew didn't think Trey heard his girlfriend as Trey bumped his shoulder into him. "Dude," Trey said as they walked down the hall together.

Drew's eyes widened at the unexpected contact. "*We should tell him how horrible his girlfriend is!*" Panda insisted. "Why did you do that?" Drew asked, deciding to talk about a different topic.

"Oh, you mean being the best wingman ever?" Trey gave him a wide grin. "You're welcome."

Drew suppressed a smile. He didn't want to encourage Trey. Drew didn't deny that he thought Miranda was pretty.

He also knew he had no game. "*Very true,*" Panda confirmed. But Drew wasn't sure if he was comfortable with Trey's involvement. "*What if Trey thinks we're a loser and we have to have his help?*" Panda's shoulders slumped at the thought.

"She is Syd's best friend, though," Trey took on a serious tone, "so…" Drew turned to his broad friend. Trey didn't need to finish his sentence, but Panda did. "*Be careful Miranda isn't crazy like Sydney AND don't break Miranda's heart, therefore unleashing Sydney's crazy.*"

"Got it," Drew said with clarity. The two parted ways and Drew's fleeting happiness slowly fizzled out as he faced the rest of his classes.

Biology and Math class passed by somewhat quickly. Nothing alerted Panda to bother Drew. Although he did have a random question here and there during Drew's diligent note taking. "*If you had to guess how many licks it took to get to the center of a Tootsie Pop, how many would it be? I think seven hundred thirty-two. Do you remember smelling Miranda's shampoo whenever her head shifted? What was that smell…strawberry? You should try to focus more. If we get our Math homework done now, then tonight we only have the English reading homework, Spanish vocab, and History class reading. I don't think elephants can jump. The only homework left after tonight would be the Econ project on Saturday.*"

Where should we take Evie for dinner? We'll probably need to stay out again tonight trying to sell off the rest of our gear."

Drew took in Panda's important comments. He liked to treat Evie to dinner on Fridays if his mom was working. Drew took every opportunity to spoil his sister. Plus, it was a good way to get out of the house for an hour or two.

When the bell released him from Math class, he headed to his locker. He felt like a buoy in the crowded hallway, drifting among the sea of students. His classmates pushed him along like a strong current. With his head buried deep in his locker, he didn't notice Wynter sneak up on him.

"Hey!" she spoke loudly over the horde.

"Hey," Drew nodded his head. *"Is she still mad at us?"* Panda peered around Drew to look at her. Avoiding her eyes, Drew stared into his locker a moment longer, making sure he had everything he needed for the weekend before he closed it and turned on his heel.

Wynter kept pace beside him. "Headed over to Evie?"

"Yeah,"

"Can I join you?"

Drew looked sideways at her and felt for his earbuds in his pocket. There they were, ready to help him begin his dissociative journey to re-collect his energy before spending the evening at home. "What about seventh?" he asked. He had a free period, but didn't want her to get in trouble for skipping.

She shrugged, "It's P.E. I'll make up the mile on Monday at lunch."

Panda shook his head in disapproval. "Are you sure?"

"I'm sure." Wynter nodded. "Well? Can I?"

They paused in the middle of the hallway as it slowly cleared. Everyone had less than a minute left to get to class on time.

"Depends…" Panda started skeptically, still a little hurt from their argument earlier. "Are you still salty?" Drew gripped his backpack strap.

Wynter's eyes slightly narrowed as she looked up at him. "I just don't want you to mess up again. Ya know?"

Drew did know. Panda knew she was right. Besides Trey, Wynter was his best friend. She visited him during his house arrest last year and she had stayed with him the longest at his dad's wake. "*Geez, last year was rough.*" She didn't say anything about his scars when she accidentally noticed his shirt ride up during an out-of-hand tickle fight. She was the one who let him borrow her notes and even copy her homework from time to time. She also kept him annoyingly accountable. He guessed she'd earned the right to worry about him. Panda hummed in thought, "*Wynter is pretty awesome.*" Drew's eyes lingered on her necklace for a moment. A green, plastic gem was cradled comfortably at the base of her neck. His face hardened as he stared at it. That green tempted to pull him into a memory, reminding him why he hated the color so much. Panda was quick to get rid of the flashback. "*Not today, Satan!*" Drew forced himself to look back at her face.

"I get it." He agreed. "I'm sorry, too," Drew grumbled out.

Wynter's lips curled up playfully. "Let me get my stuff from my locker and we can head over to her school."

Drew nodded and quietly walked over to her locker. Panda ran laps back and forth, anxious they would be late getting Evie.

To Drew's and Panda's relief, they weren't late.

CHAPTER FIVE

"I love your hair, Evie," Wynter complimented.

"Thank you! Drew did it." Evie dangled herself off the kitchen counter like it was a set of monkey bars. She watched her brother wash a handful of grapes for her afternoon snack. If he wasn't paying attention, she'd eat the whole bag in one sitting. This was their normal routine after school. With his mom and Liam at work, Drew was left to take care of Evie.

"It looks great," Wynter responded, simultaneously complimenting Drew as she smiled down at Evie and looked up at him. Panda blushed at her praise. As she sat on the barstool, Wynter watched the siblings, wishing with a sad heart that she and her older sister were that close.

Drew shrugged dismissively. "I don't know a whole lot."

"Do you know how to cornrow?"

Panda snorted. "Of course not!" Drew chuckled under his breath.

"Evie," Wynter leaned over the counter, "do you want me to show you a new hair style?"

"Yeah!" Evie stopped dangling and jumped up and down.

"What about homework?" Drew protested.

"It's Friday," she skipped in place, "I don't have any."

"How'd you do on your vocab test?"

"I missed one," she mumbled.

"Oh no," Wynter sympathized.

"Which one?" Drew patted dry the plump, green fruit.

Her button nose scrunched up in frustration. "Straight."

"Hmmm, that is a tough one. We'll work on it a bit this weekend." Panda snapped his fingers at Drew, reminding him about their plans with Miranda. "Oh, Evie," Drew held the bowl close to him. Her wide eyes focused on the little hostages. "I've got to go to a friend's house tomorrow to work on homework. She's got a sister. And lots of toys for you to play with. Wanna come with?"

Her eyes slanted when she recognized the favor. Her head tilted to the side. "What if I don't like it?"

"Then we leave," Panda said protectively. Drew agreed, "Simple." Evie squinted her eyes even more in challenge. He passed her the bowl, sternly, "I promise."

Like a gremlin, she took the bowl and scurried off downstairs. Wynter watched Drew with skepticism. "What friend?"

"Oh," he grabbed his bag and followed his sister down to his room with Wynter close behind. "Miranda."

Evie plopped herself on his futon couch and turned on his TV.

Panda helped Drew kick his clothes into one corner, attempting to tidy up his room, only now clean was mixed with dirty. "*Mom's going to be pissed when we give her our laundry. She can tell at a glance which ones are clean. She'll probably just accuse us of being too lazy to put them away again,*" Panda chastised. Drew sat down on his bed and began to cocoon himself with his homework. He had five problems left in math. He decided he'd tackle that first while it was still somewhat fresh.

"Miranda GOODMAN?!" Drew completely missed Wynter's shock as her brow raised.

"*This won't end well.*" Panda's stomach tightened hearing her tone. "Yeah," Drew said, keeping his eyes on his Math homework. "We've got an Econ project together."

"Wyn," Evie turned to her with chipmunk-like cheeks

stuffed with grapes. "Can we play salon now?"

"Of course," Wynter stood up to head to the bathroom. "Let me get the stuff."

Drew and Panda released a collective sigh. "*Think we dodged a fight?*" Panda was doubtful. "*How could we forget how much Wynter hates Miranda too?*" Wynter came back with a spray bottle full of hot water, the comb, a hand towel, and a few hair ties. Evie plopped down on the floor and nestled herself between Wynter's legs, contently enjoying her grapes and her talking horses show. Wynter got to work, being gentle with Evie's tender head. Panda cowered behind Drew, fearful of upsetting Wynter. "*Be careful, dude.*"

"You know, Goodman and Porter are the ones who started that rumor last year."

Drew packed up his Math homework, ready to get a head start on his Spanish. Wynter's experienced hands weaved Evie's hair down her head.

"Porter I could see but I don't know about…"

"They're both culpable, Drew!" Wynter's offended eyes snapped to him.

Drew chewed the inside of his cheek. "It's just a project, Wyn."

"Why aren't you partners with Trey? Aren't you guys in

that class together?"

Drew sighed, frustrated that he upset Wynter. "He's working with Porter."

Wynter clucked her tongue and shook her head. She resumed her work on the right side of Evie's head. "It's bad enough Trey chose Porter's side. But be my guest if you want to work with that…" she paused, remembering that seven-year-old ears were snuggled between her knees, "…Witch!" Wynter hissed through gritted teeth.

"*Maybe working with Miranda isn't such a good idea.*" Panda scratched at his furry chin. "*But I don't understand why she hates Miranda so much. She seems nice to me.*"

Drew spent the rest of the evening working on his homework while Wynter played video games with Evie. Evie loved her new hairdo. She already coined them as "caterpillars." Drew felt plenty of pressure from Panda to learn the new technique after seeing how happy his baby sister was. Wynter's mood improved the more time she spent with Evie. Panda watched them with admiration as Drew focused on finishing all his homework for the weekend.

"Drew," Evie sighed dramatically. Her character on the TV made cute poses as it waited for their player to take control again. Wynter's character kept roaming, absorbed in her current side mission.

"Yeah, Eves?"

"I'm hungry."

Drew skimmed for a good stopping spot in his History class book and then slammed it closed dramatically. He plopped it beside him in the pile of his other work, feeling like it was close enough for now. Panda was quiet and Drew suddenly felt playful. He stretched, groaned, and made wild noises, trying to make Evie laugh. She giggled loudly as Drew rolled onto his belly, inches from his sister as she leaned over the arm of the futon.

"What ya want?"

Her lips curled inward. "Pizza?"

"Yeah, you want pizza?" He asked her doubtfully. She squealed out a yes as Drew scooped her up onto his bed. Her giggles turned inaudible as Drew tickled her sides ruthlessly. He paused a moment so she could breathe. "Put your shoes back on and we'll head out."

She didn't need any further instruction. Bolting off the bed, she slipped her shoes back on and ran up the stairs. She screamed down the stairwell for them to hurry up. Wynter chuckled at Evie's level of puppy energy, and powered off the systems. Drew quickly slipped his own shoes on and grabbed his backpack.

Normally, Evie and Drew biked down to the pizzeria, but Wynter didn't have her bike so they walked alongside Evie while she weaved wavy patterns on the sidewalk with her bike tires. Drew was thankful for the bright evening. Summer was just three weeks away. He worried how he would keep Evie occupied if he was going to make money during the season. Summer was the best time to sell. Kids looking to party into the long night and tourists coming and going made it easy. Panda regrettably hoped Evie had a friend she could spend most of her time with. He loved his little sister, but babysitting was a challenge at times.

Panda was pleasantly quiet as he eavesdropped on Drew's conversation with Wynter.

"You going to tell me why you ditched seventh?" Drew finally asked after a few minutes.

Wynter shrugged. "You know I switch to my dad's every other week." Drew nodded in answer. She always started her week with him on a Sunday. "I guess I just didn't want to go home to an empty house."

Drew pushed his lips to the side. "Your mom and stepdad out of town again?"

"Yup. They're at some stupid beach in California for the weekend." She scoffed in anger. "Oh," she turned to Drew, "and guess where they've decided to vacation this summer?" Drew didn't guess. He let his friend vent. "They're going on a freaking cruise! Can you get any more bougie? And without me! They didn't even ask if I wanted to go."

Drew felt bad for Wynter. Her mom and stepdad acted like empty nesters ever since Wynter's older sister went to college last year. Wynter still had another year at home before she'd be leaving for college. *"She'll be leaving sooner if she gets into the transfer program,"* Panda reminded him bitterly. Drew wondered if maybe that was why she applied. She'd have her own chance to experience the world. It wasn't like her parents were taking her with them.

"You'll be on your own all summer?" Drew asked in concern.

Wynter shook her head. "I'll be at my dad's. But you know how he is. So laid back he doesn't care what I get up to."

Drew had met her dad a few times. He didn't mind whenever Drew and Trey came over, so long as her door stayed open, of course. Her dad never seemed to ask what they had planned for the day. And she never got in trouble on the rare occasion they dropped her off past her curfew. Drew made a mental note to spend as much time with Wynter as possible this summer. That way, they could assuage each other's loneliness and log quality time in case she moved around the world from him.

With some protest from Wynter, Drew bought three slices of pizza, one for each of them. They enjoyed their meal on the curb outside the restaurant. As the sun began to set, the street turned hazy like a nineties home movie. The colors became warmer, muted. Evie was in her own world as she slightly swayed her head from side to side, her happy dance whenever she ate. The evening was nearly perfect. And then Panda jabbed Drew in his side. He turned in time to see one of their classmates approaching. Drew's spine straightened. He didn't want to do this now. *Not with Evie here.*

"Drew," the newcomer said in a slurred, lazy drawl. "Sup Wynter."

Wynter nodded her head at him while she squinted in displeasure.

"Zac," Drew acknowledged him. Zac leaned in close and pulled Drew's rigid body into a half-attempted hug. The skinny teen sat down beside him. Evie looked pensive as she observed the stranger. Wynter thankfully distracted her.

"You'll have to thank her later." Panda made a memo.

"Don't touch me, Zac." Drew ordered in a hard tone. *"Make this quick,"* Panda agreed.

Zac blew a raspberry in front of him. "So touchy, brah."

"What do you want, dude?" Drew took a bite of his pizza, growing impatient of this conversation already. *"Why did it have to be Zac?"* Panda groaned.

Zac ran his hand across his nose, followed by a hard sniff. His eyes looked sunken in. Heavy bags weighed down his youthful face. "You got any Percs?"

Drew waved him off. "I have the same shit as always, Zac. Go find Kurt if you want extra."

"Oh dude, don't be like that. You know how Kurt can be," Zac said under his breath. "What kind of weed you got?" He wrung his hands like he desperately wanted something else.

Drew gave him a bored expression. Drew often felt like he was stuck in a loop when he talked to Zac. He only ever had weed and uppers. Why was that so complicated for Zac to remember?

"Fine," Zac sighed, rolling his eyes dramatically. "Can I get some Indica?"

Drew promptly dug into his backpack as Zac dove into

his own pocket. Wynter watched the exchange of drugs and money out the corner of her eye as Evie chattered away to her. Drew heard Evie stutter with food in her mouth. Zac left after mumbling, "Thanks."

Drew kept his eyes straight ahead, squinting hard as the sun reflected off a sign into them. Guilt squeezed his stomach into a tight ball. He was a product of his classmate's downfall, and he had exposed his little sister to it. Panda let him know when Wynter wasn't looking at him anymore. He could only handle one critic at a time.

CHAPTER SIX

Drew snored hard into his pillow. Panda slept on top of him. He always found it hard to initially slip into oblivion when Panda weighed on him like that, like a pile of wet clothes smothering him. But once Drew managed to succumb to subconsciousness, he slept like a rock.

"Drew…Drew…"

Someone was shaking his arm with more force. His eyes snapped open. He sniffed hard. The inside of his nose burned at the sudden inhalation. He looked around in a panic for a moment. "*What's going on?!*" Panda's head swiveled in equal panic. Evie's wide, chestnut eyes stared at Drew with serenity, waiting for him to find his grounding.

Panda groaned, rolled off Drew and burrowed his head into the pillow. "What's up, Eves?" Drew swallowed as his heart rate slowed.

She leaned in close to his face. "Mom's making waffles." The sharp smell of milk rolled out her mouth.

"Mom's home?"

Panda laughed bitterly, "She thinks pancakes can make up for her absenteeism."

"Waffles," Evie corrected.

"*Shit…did I say that out loud?*" Panda slapped a hand over his mouth. Drew's head felt heavy as he slightly lifted it. With squinted eyes, he stared at his sister for a moment. Her face didn't change from the selfless patience she gave him. "Alright, I'll be up there in a minute."

She leaned onto the bed a few times, jumped in place, and then ran upstairs. Her happy steps trailed down through the ceiling. Other steps Drew could now hear also made their way into his room. He rolled over onto his back. With an annoyed groan, he rubbed the heel of his hand roughly into his eyes.

"*At least they're waffles,*" Panda cheerfully mocked. He shoved Drew out of the bed.

With a good stretch, he found his black jeans and threw on a clean shirt. Wandering to the bathroom, he quickly rinsed his face and brushed his teeth. The scent of Saturday morning breakfast wafted up his nose the more he staggered up the stairs.

"Hey dude," Liam gave him a plastic smile. "Want some coffee?"

"I'll get it myself," Drew grumbled, brushing past him.

"Morning, hon," his mom gave him too wide of a smile that early in the morning as she briefly moved her eyes to look at him.

Her attention quickly returned to serving Evie, eyes cast down. Drew carefully worked around his uncle to get his coffee. It was like Liam purposefully took up too much space, and got in Drew's way. Satisfied with his mug, Drew walked over to the dining table and sat beside Evie at her normal spot at the end. He propped his head on the table with his hand, but couldn't deny how good everything looked as his stomach grumbled.

"Want me to fix your plate?" his mom offered.

Panda salivated. "Sure," Drew nodded.

His mom scooped a healthy amount of scrambled eggs, sausages, and waffles on his plate. He helped himself to a few strawberries that were on the side before Evie claimed the whole bowl. A tired thank you passed his mouth. Panda got a bit carried away as he drizzled everything in syrup. His mom bit back a comment about the disgusting amount of syrup on her son's plate. Instead, she smiled fleetingly across the table at him.

Liam sat down beside his mom. Panda stuffed his face as Drew sipped on his coffee. He threw a wink at Evie when she stared at him a moment too long. She snickered behind her fork, thinking his large mouthfuls were funny.

Awkward silence and the sound of scraping of plates filled the room. The occasional mourning dove interjected. Tumble weeds could have drifted by on the vacant plate set at the other head of the table.

"Any plans today?" His mom broke the silence. She looked expectantly between the three of them.

Liam shrugged, "I'm going to stop by the shop for a few hours. Make sure everyone is doing ok..."

"Are you working today?" Panda bulldozed over Liam. Drew looked directly at his mom.

She stammered for a moment. "I'm working later this evening, but I should be home tonight, and I've got all day tomorrow off." Evie kicked her legs excitedly, but Drew was far from impressed. *"Sure, that's her plan. But what if they need her to work a double?"* Panda doubted. Drew never put much stock in his mom's schedule. "There's a new group coming in so I should be able to get my flexible hours back. Weekends and the evenings at home," his mom sounded hopeful.

"*Yeah right*," Panda scoffed. Drew just bit his tongue and gave his mother a rigid nod.

Her eyes betrayed her forced smile. With a distraught gaze, she longingly reached over the table toward her son. He might as well have been miles away, he felt so distant. She had no idea what was happening in his life anymore. And Drew didn't give her an inch to work with. His uncle resumed talking, but Drew tuned it out, not caring what Liam had to say. Drew didn't succumb to his mom's pitiful look and shifted his attention to his plate. It was a battlefield of scattered eggs, half chewed on sausages, and waffles drowning in syrup like dinosaurs trapped in tar.

His stomach started to churn and voices drifted in and out like wind whistling through a hollow space. Drew heard Evie talk about her hair. Glowing brightly, she praised Wynter for her new hairstyle. The caterpillars now looked like a frizzy mess. Of course, his mom knew how to recreate the cornrows. She was just never around to do them for Evie. Celeste promised Evie she would re-do the cornrows before she went to work. It sounded more like begging to Panda. A desperate need to reconnect.

With a clenched jaw, Drew watched his mom as she spoke to Evie. The dark skin around her eyes looked even darker. Exhaustion had bruised the thin skin. She was wearing a clean pair of pajamas as if she hadn't slept in them the night before. Who knew how fresh those pajamas were? How many nights did she spend in hospital rooms tending to strangers she grew closer to in her rounds than her own children? Her black, braided hair, was concealed in a tightly wrapped, colorful silk scarf. Drew had faint memories of admiring her flamboyant head wraps when he was Evie's age. The extravagant bows his mom made astounded him. He watched her long, skinny fingers carefully holding her fork, then her mug, and imagined that her fingers were inhumanely cold to the touch.

Sterile.

Subzero.

Panda's eyes wandered to the empty chair at the head of the table. The chair hadn't been touched in months. Even Trey and Wynter knew better than to occupy that space, for fear of sitting on the lap of a phantom. "*I miss him*," Panda echoed softly. Not wanting to dwell in the pool of grief that morning, Drew looked away.

Emerald green eyes stared back at him.

His father's twin sat beside his mother. When Drew was younger, he thought it was cool his dad had a twin. Now, it was like a plot point in a horror movie. The ultimate creep factor. They had the same hair color. Sandy brown. But Liam's was longer, like a 90s surfer douche bag. He kept it long enough to tuck behind his ears. Drew's dad always kept his hair short, and his face clean-shaven, as opposed to his short-bearded uncle. Liam had his father beat by muscle, though. He was more defined, leaner. Both were six feet tall, dwarfing his mother who was five, five. *"And a half,"* Panda corrected.

Drew's long legs bounced with unease. He was already six feet himself. But he felt like he hadn't exactly grown into his long limbs yet. *"Our body is awkward,"* Panda complained self-consciously. He wondered how tall Evie would grow to be. Liam's cream-colored skin tightened around the eyes as Drew maintained eye contact. Sharing space with his uncle made his skin crawl. *"I need space,"* Panda pleaded. *"I can't stand it!"*

Drew wordlessly stood up and grabbed his plate. Panda was ready to make his way downstairs. His heart pounded.

His mom paused in what she was saying, "Are you done already?"

"Yeah," Drew said. He put his drowning food out of its misery and dumped it in the trash. "I've got some homework to finish up and then I've got to figure out what I'm doing with Miranda." Panda immediately slapped himself on the forehead, irritated that Drew had let her name slip out.

"Miranda?" Liam started.

"Who's Miranda?" His mom cocked her head to the side in curiosity.

Drew turned to look at his mom over the kitchen counter. His face tightened as he realized that he had his uncle's attention too. "*Just ignore him,*" Panda advised.

Drew cleared his throat. Looking only at his mom, he replied, "She's my project partner."

His mom nodded, "What's the project?"

"Econ," he sighed. "We have to make an investment plan." He lifted his hand and gestured to his little sister, "I was planning on bringing Evie with me." Drew licked his lips. The leftover sweetness from the syrup caused his stomach to lurch. He swallowed hard. "Miranda has a little sister Evie can play with."

"It's ok for you to go Drew," Liam spoke calmly, looking between him and his mom, "but I think Celeste might've wanted to spend some time with you both today." Liam bit his bottom lip as he tried to speak for Drew's mom.

Panda crossed his arms and leaned against the wall, directing hostility toward their uncle. His anger started to boil. He questioned why he even tried to hide from Liam in the first place. "*This jerk is in our house! How dare he act like this!*" Panda raged. "I didn't know you'd be home today, Mom," Drew tried to speak evenly around Panda's irritation. He brought his eyes back to his mother, "I thought it'd be good for Evie to have a friend."

"That's well and good Drew," his mom nodded in agreeance, "but I don't know this…what was her name? Miranda? I haven't met her mom yet. It'd be different if you were paired with Wynter."

Drew resisted the urge to roll his eyes, "Wyn isn't in my class. Miranda is really nice, Mom."

"I'm sure she is," his mom's tone turned parental. "You don't have to watch her, hon. Liam and I will be here."

"*What if she has to run to work early?*" Panda whispered in Drew's ear. His fur tickled Drew's face as paranoia leached into his system. "*She'd never understand,*" Panda continued. "*We have to keep Evie safe.*"

"I don't mind watching her." Drew took on a pleading look with his mom, hoping it was enough to convince her to let Evie go with him.

"If I may, Celeste," Liam put his hand on his mom's shoulder. "*No, you may not,*" Panda growled. With his mom's approving nod, he continued, "I'm not sure how much I trust Drew to be alone with Evie."

"Excuse me?!" Panda snapped. Panda clenched his hands tight, struggling to keep his anger below the surface.

"You were caught selling drugs last summer, Drew," his uncle asserted. "I don't trust the crowd you keep. I don't think that'll be good for Evie."

"Evie is safe with me," Drew retorted in a sharp tone. "*Safer with me than with you!*" Panda affirmed.

He looked to his mom for support, but his heart sank as she avoided his pleading face. His mom was on Liam's side. Drew's composure grew rigid as he suddenly felt attacked.

"When were you planning on being back?" Celeste's question surprised Drew.

He shrugged, "I don't know. A couple hours."

"Does she live around here?"

Drew nodded.

"I want you both home by two," his mom said in compromise. Liam called Celeste's name in protest, but she ignored him. "I want Miranda's address and an update every hour. You tell me when you get there and when you're coming back."

"Ok," Drew said quietly. His ego felt severely bruised and tired. He swiftly turned and headed down the stairs before his scrutinizing mother could say anything more.

Panda paced around the room. His hands combed through the soft fur on his head. *"What an asshole,"* he muttered. *"Can you believe the balls on Liam! Saying Evie wasn't safe with us! US!"*

Drew was plenty angry with his uncle. But the look of disbelief on his mom's face was what haunted him the most. She didn't trust him.

"And mom isn't any better," Panda continued to rant. *"Like making breakfast and imposing family time suddenly makes us the damned Brady Bunch!"*

Drew sat on the edge of his bed and smeared the palms of his hands on his pants. His leg bounced wildly with adrenaline. He stared at his backpack, knowing the contents were a jumbled contradiction: school work to try to be a functioning member of society snuggled closely with illegally obtained Adderall, Ritalin, Percocet, and weed to sell to his peers who were just trying to get by like he was. Drew swiftly lost the motivation to read the last chapter he needed to be fully caught up in History class.

Panda kept pacing. "*Let's punch the wall!*"

"And break my hand?" Drew shook his head. "No way."

"*Can I punch you then?*"

Drew looked at Panda with increasing fury, "No!"

"*Scream into a pillow?*" Panda suggested halfheartedly. The idea sounded babyish to both their ears. "*Oh!*" he exclaimed with this new idea. He kneeled in front of Drew. "*Real quick.*" He panted like a junkie. "*I was thinking on your hip.*"

Drew stared at him with vacancy. "What are you talking about?"

"*Just a little cut? On your hip. Please?*"

Drew shoved Panda away with disgust at the thought. Panda had cut up Drew's skin in a frenzy when he was thirteen. Drew had resisted the urge until he caved last year. Number seventeen on his hip. Drew instantly regretted it when it happened. He didn't feel better after Panda promised he would.

"No!"

Drew's guilt over his lack of ability to control his emotions was made worse when Evie walked in on him getting dressed a month ago. Either he failed to hear her knock or she barged in. He only had on a pair of boxers, so, she'd just seen eight of his scars. But it was more than what he'd wanted her to see. Afterwards, she didn't act any differently around him. And to both their relief and guilt, Evie never asked Drew about it. He wondered if she understood the cavernous secret she intruded upon. It was a burden more than anything and just the tip of the iceberg. He had felt exposed.

"That won't happen again," Panda cooed. *"Come on…I'll be careful."* Drew squeezed his eyes shut, shaking his head. *"It hurts so much. I know, brother. I can make it hurt less."*

"I said no!" Drew said more forcefully, shoving Panda away. Drew inhaled sharply and blinked furiously. He leaned forward on his knees and buried his face in his hands, muffling his desolation. After a moment of uncertainty, Panda started rubbing Drew's back in soothing circles.

CHAPTER SEVEN

Evie giggled as the wind whistled through her helmet straps. Her backpack held enough snacks to feed an army, courtesy of their mom. She brought a few extra dolls just in case she didn't like anything her new playmate had to offer. Drew's bag had his normal swirling paradox, mainly because he didn't trust Liam to not go through his things when he wasn't home. Panda kept reminding him about what had happened after that morning's breakfast. Drew was just happy he didn't let Panda punch or cut him like he wanted to.

Drew was surprised that they only lived a few blocks away from Miranda. It was an easy excursion on their bikes for some needed freedom. For both of them. They pulled up in front of Miranda's two-story home, a pale-yellow house with a crisp white door. Bright flowers decorated the porch.

Drew carefully propped their bikes against the porch rails. Evie made sure he didn't crush the "pretty flowers." Evie rang the doorbell while Drew sent a text to his mom letting her know they'd arrived.

An older version of Miranda opened the door with a wide, welcoming smile. "*Her mom*," Panda hid behind Drew.

"Hey guys," she pointed between the two of them, "Drew and Evie?" Her faint southern accent seemed misplaced in their area. But her tone was friendly.

Drew pulled Evie in by the shoulders with an awkward smile. "Yes, ma'am."

"Come on in," she waved them in, holding the door wider.

They stepped inside the crisp air-conditioned home that looked even bigger inside. Panda was extra quiet as he took in everything. Drew and Evie stood, gawking, in the entry-way. It looked like a showroom with freshly vacuumed carpets and everything recently dusted. All the curtains were open, letting in all the natural sunlight. It was bright enough that none of the lights were on. Drew kicked his shoes off, worried their presence would be enough of a stain on the home. Evie followed suit, looking up at the high ceiling.

Mrs. Goodman walked further into her home. An invisible tether pulled them along behind her. She paused at the stairs on the right and loudly announced the presence of guests.

Drew imagined those period piece movies his mom was obsessed with that had a stuffy announcer with ruffles craning his neck straight like a giraffe who declared a new-comer's presence. *"Drew and Evie of Sir and Lady Collins,"* Panda mocked in a bad English accent.

However, Mrs. Goodman's voice sounded more like the screech of a demanding mother that would catch the attention of all kids, whether they were related or not. The banshee turned back to them with a smooth grin. "Can I get y'all anything?"

"I'm ok, thank you." Drew forced a smile, his eyes tight.

Mrs. Goodman turned toward Evie. "What about you, darlin'? I've got juice."

Evie looked up at Drew for permission. He nodded his head in earnest. The more comfortable she felt meant the more homework he could get done. *"Don't lie to me,"* Panda whispered. *"The more comfortable she feels, the longer we can stay here. Away from home."* They trailed Mrs. Goodman to the kitchen that didn't look like it had ever been used.

"I know Drew and Miranda have the same Econ class,"

she said, with her head inside a NASA looking fridge, "but what school do you go to, Evie?" Finding what she was looking for, she passed Evie her beverage.

Panda swiftly took the juice box out of her hand and opened it for Evie. She had a habit of squirting the sugary liquid all over the place upon impact with the straw.

"Howard Elementary," Evie answered with satisfaction once her big brother opened her drink for her.

"Oh," she exclaimed. "What grade?"

"Second."

"How exciting," her cheeks pulled back. "Ah," she waved over her youngest who seemed like a smaller version of Miranda, only with curlier chocolate hair and rounder, baby-fat cheeks. "You and Maddison go to the same school. Maddy here is in third grade right now."

Evie waved at her, sucking on her straw with utter contentment. Maddy looked at the ground for a moment in discomfort. Mrs. Goodman squatted down to their level. "Maddy, this is Evie. Why don't y'all go play for a bit." Maddy looked at her mom with desperate eyes, quietly begging her mom to not force her to play host. Mrs. Goodman's eyes hardened for a moment. "Go outside and play."

Evie stared at Maddison with expectation. She confidently drank from her juice box. Wide eyed, she waited for Maddison to make the first move. Drew observed the difference between the girls as Maddison's leg twitched. She seemed eager to run away. Drew would kill to have Evie's confidence.

Maddison shrugged, losing the wordless fight with her mom, "Come on." Maddy turned and threw her whole, small body into sliding the glass door open, and led them outside to the backyard. Evie quietly followed, her bag armed with snacks and toys strapped to her back.

"Cute kid," the slim brunette stood up. Cropped wavy curls hovered just above her shoulders. She crossed her skinny arms to look at Drew. His eyes remained on the playhouse in the backyard. "How's your mom doing?"

"*Why?*" Panda questioned, his guard going up. "She's good," Drew lied. He actually had no idea how his mom was doing. "*Is that bad? Does that make us a bad son? Probably.*" Panda muttered.

She pressed her lips into a thin smile and nodded. "I've been meaning to reach out and all after...since your dad, uh..." She chewed her bottom lip as Drew played dumb. He was curious to see how deep she'd dig her hole. "I'm going to go see what's keeping Miranda." She snapped her fingers toward the stairs.

Once Mrs. Goodman disappeared up the stairs, Drew exhaled for the first time since Evie had rang the doorbell.

"*OH MY GOD!*" Panda slouched, resting his hands on his knees. "*That was weird, right?*"

Drew just hummed in response to him. He scratched at the back of his head. He really didn't know what to do right now. Stay inside and wait for Miranda? Or keep an eye on the kids? Not giving a shit, he walked outside. He sat down at the patio table, protected by the outdoor umbrella. Through slanted eyes, he watched as Maddy slowly warmed up to his baby sister. Their quiet conversation soon evolved into running around the playhouse in a fit of laughter. His heart twanged with a deep ache.

Evie didn't ever get a chance to play like this on the weekend. Well, with anyone her age anyways. There was only so much Drew could do with their ten-year age gap. "*Is that our fault?*" Panda wondered.

"*By the way…*" Panda started. Drew hated when he started sentences like that. "*Is now a good time to point out how weird it is to hang out with Miranda knowing it upsets Wynter?*"

Drew tilted his head toward Panda, "No, it's not a good time."

"But I kind of believe Wynter. What if Miranda did help Porter start those rumors? Does this make us a bad friend?" Panda gasped, *"Treason! Friendship treason of the highest order!"*

"Not treason," Drew tried to soothe. "It's just a project."

"Yeah right, and not just an in with a girl you've had a crush on since seventh grade," Panda retorted.

The sound of the sliding glass door opening beside him made him jump and silenced his conversation with Panda. A smile not too old, not too young, but just right greeted him. Panda squealed with excitement like a girl. Or maybe that was the seven-year-old just ten feet away from him. He didn't really want to check. Panda made Drew launch up on his feet before he could really process why he was standing up. Drew tried not to stare, even though Panda begged him to.

Miranda half waved at him as she found a seat beside him. Her lacy, white sundress kicked at her knees as she scurried behind him. The breeze gave him a small sniff of her shampoo or perfume. Drew really didn't care what it was. It just smelled like strawberries. Her dark hair was up in a high ponytail, which exposed her porcelain neck.

"Sorry about that. I had my door closed. I didn't know you guys were here." She shyly tried to brush stray hairs behind her ear.

"Oh," Drew shrugged, "that's ok." Panda was shocked, *"How could she not hear her mom screaming at her?"*

They sat in silence for a moment. Miranda bashfully placed her hands under her legs. Drew scratched at his arm. His eyes followed Evie.

"Should we…uh…" Miranda paused for a half a second. Drew's and Panda's attention snapped to her. Her smile faltered a moment under the intensity. "Should we get started?"

"Yes, absolutely." He sat up more, thankful to be moving in some type of direction.

"Do you want to work out here or go back inside?" She pointed at the sliding glass door.

Drew's eyes squinted for a moment at her question. But not from the sun. His hearing focused on the laughter behind him.

Miranda's eyes were soft with understanding. "Here is ok. I'm just going to grab my stuff."

Drew nodded. The corner of her dress brushed at his arm as she walked by. Panda gasped for air. Drew's heart skipped a beat. When she was gone, Panda smacked him upside the head. *"Dude! I think she wanted to show you her room! God! Why are you such a loser?"*

"Would you knock it off!" Drew huffed, rubbing the back of his head. "We're here for the stupid project. Nothing else."

"No, of course not." Panda rocked a little in his chair. *"Why would she want us when every guy in school drooled over her? We're a nobody."* Drew pulled his notebook and pen out of his bag as Panda continued to belittle him.

His phone buzzed in his pocket. It was Celeste, no doubt, checking on them. Drew watched as Evie played house with Maddy. When he called out her name, it looked like he had violently brought her back to reality. Evie answered, rather annoyed that he had interrupted them. Confirming she was doing just fine, Drew shot his mom a quick text that they were doing ok.

Miranda came back with a bottle of water, her notebook, an assortment of pens, and her laptop. "Did you want something to drink or anything?"

"I'm good, thanks." Drew attempted to smile. *"Nope!"* Panda criticized from beside the playhouse, checking on Evie. *"I can see your smile from here. It's weird. Quit it."* Drew dropped his smile.

"So, we've got to set up a ten-year investment plan," she

spoke as she opened her computer. "Any ideas on where to start?"

"A budget?"

"Ohhhhhh!" Drew's stomach flipped at Miranda's excitement. "Good idea!" His heart quickened at hearing her praise.

They kept working for a solid hour outside. Mrs. Goodman occasionally popped her head outside to ask if they needed anything. Miranda's smile tightened as she answered. Panda noticed that Mrs. Goodman left the glass door open and the screen door closed. Knowing that the girls' laughter and Miranda's and his words about their project drifted inside to the kitchen, Panda contemplated, *"Do you think she's eavesdropping?"*

At some point, Drew found himself relaxing in Miranda's company, even enjoying the occasional distraction from their sisters. Evie and Maddy kept bringing them flowers, expanding on their imaginary town and pretending the patio table was the flower shop. After an hour, Mrs. Goodman asked the girls to move inside to play.

Drew thought that Maddison would probably get sunburned if she stayed out any longer, but Evie's skin would just get darker, absorbing the sun and reflecting a tan darker than her natural copper tone. Drew and Panda trusted that Evie was comfortable with Maddison. If not, Evie would have already told Drew that she was ready to leave. But Panda was being overprotective, so Drew kept asking if Evie was ok. Each time Evie answered with a wide smile and a strong head nod. Panda still wanted to keep an eye on her, so when the girls went inside, Drew and Miranda moved inside too. The girls played in Maddy's room with the door wide open. Drew had a clear view from Miranda's room across the hall.

But being in Miranda's room made him nervous again.

"I'm telling you dude, she likes us!" Panda's hope mounted at the possibility Miranda found Drew attractive. Drew had never had a girlfriend. *"Your withdrawn behavior is a turn-off,"* Panda told him.

The only other girl's room he'd been in was Wynter's. And Miranda's room was dramatically different than Wynter's. Wynter's walls were covered with various retro rock bands and anime posters. To the point that there wasn't a speck of the white walls poking through. All her furniture and décor were dark. Black if she could help it. And Wynter tended to be a bit disorganized. She was the smartest person Drew knew, but her room was always a mess whenever he came over. He could never point out what a disaster her room was because that would make him a hypocrite.

Miranda's room was the polar opposite. Her walls were painted pastel pink. Some of the most beautiful paintings Drew had ever seen were on the wall. Twenty combinations of a forest collaged the space. Some with a lake. Others with a footpath or mountains. Most covered in nothing but trees. Rainy. Foggy. Snow covered. Bright sunshine. Bathed in moonlight. Vibrant natural greens and browns. Or one hazy color. Different opacities treated like a whole palette of paint. Yellow. Purple. Pink. White. Black. Gray. A particular blue forest called to Drew. He felt submerged in a Bob Ross gallery.

A humongous, white vanity, which Drew assumed she used mostly as a desk for homework rather than grooming herself, took up her other wall space. The mirror was framed with lights and pictures. Polaroid photos of the cheer squad and one-on-one photos of Miranda and Sydney Porter made him uneasy. He imagined Porter playing dress up with Miranda in front of that oval mirror.

Her twin bed was made with crisp folds. He felt out of place in the neat room. Not wanting to disturb the girlie innocence, he grabbed her desk chair and sat in it backward.

He crossed his arms, leaned forward, and perched his chin on his arms. He swung slightly in the swivel, his eyes unable to leave those paintings. Panda sat awkwardly in the middle of the room, drawing patterns into the stiff carpet. His eyes ping-ponged back and forth between Drew and Miranda, cataloging every moment. Miranda sat on the edge of her bed with her laptop neatly placed on her knees. Panda scooted over closer to Drew and then spotted Mrs. Goodman out of the corner of his eye, checking on everyone again. She gave Drew a polite smile and disappeared.

Miranda went over their investment plan, recapping what they'd decided to do. Drew quietly hummed in agreement. He felt uncomfortable in this new environment. Outside, he felt relaxed, unrestricted by her sunny backyard. Inside though… "*In her room,*" Panda was still astonished. The AC burned Drew's nostrils. Goosebumps crawled up his bare arms. His stomach flip-flopped being in her intimate space. This was the same space where she slept. "*Got dressed…got naked,*" Panda pointed out.

Miranda's nose flared when she detected the change in Drew's mood. "Well, I'd say we got the bulk done," she shrugged. "That leaves research on the investment strategy and putting the presentation together. And, of course…

practicing the presentation," she tacked on with the roll of her eyes.

Drew stared at her, biting the inside of his cheek.

She pushed her lips to the side in thought. "I was thinking doing a PowerPoint might be easier," she continued. "Did you want to work on it now or later?" Miranda watched him carefully.

"*Now!*" Panda swatted at Drew's leg in urgency. "*Let's stay in her room longer! Maybe she wants to hook up with us. This has got the be our destiny. Why else would she want to be your partner?*"

Drew tried to swallow. His throat was suddenly dry from Panda's growing excitement. He looked down the hall. Evie looked like she forgot Drew was even there. He pulled his phone out. Seeing a text from Celeste, he checked the time. Clearing his throat, Drew nodded his head. "We have to be home in an hour. We can work on it now if you're up for it."

For thirty minutes, they got the outline of their PowerPoint done. Panda stared, mouth open and speechless when Drew found himself sitting beside Miranda on the bed. "*Put your arm around her!*" Drew ignored Panda's suggestion and watched Miranda's dainty fingers with admiration as they flew across the keyboard with such precision. He couldn't even type without looking down at the keyboard. As Miranda explained the outline of their presentation, Drew noticed just how close he really was sitting next to her. The space was already small given the twin bed. "*There's no way this bed can fit the two of us.*" Panda shook his head as he tried to imagine them on it. "*Or in it.*"

Feeling mortified and a little disgusted at his train of thought, Drew scooted away a bit. Miranda was too trusting and good natured to be Drew's partner. Surely, she'd heard the rumors around school about what his home life was like. "*That you're a loser drug dealer.*" And here he was, fantasizing about hooking up with her when she was just being nice and offered to be his partner. "*What a pervert!*" Panda changed his tune and accused Drew.

Luckily, Evie was ready to leave when Drew decided it was time for them to leave. Celeste had just sent another text. She was getting antsy that they had thirty minutes to get home. Miranda and Drew agreed to meet up again next weekend. By then, most of their research should be done. Or at least, Drew hoped so. He'd have to work in the library during lunch to catch up. He didn't have a computer at home and wasn't able to stay during seventh or after school, so that meant lunch was his only free time.

Drew noticed that the playdate had really worn Evie out. Her stride beside him was a snail's pace. He decided he would bring Evie home on his bike and come back for her bike after he dropped her off. Drew shoved her bag inside of his backpack so it would be less for him to carry. He then strapped his bag on the front of his chest. Miranda watched them with concern, not thinking this was a safe idea.

Evie expertly stepped onto the back of his bike pegs. It wasn't her favorite way to travel, but she was too tired to argue. Drew carefully balanced them as her grip around his waist tightened. She rested her cheek against his shoulder as he cautiously put his left foot on one of the pedals.

"What are y'all doin'?" Mrs. Goodman's shrill voice caused Drew to wobble a bit on his bike. Drew looked up at the worried parent.

"Evie's too tired to ride her bike home. I was going to come back and grab it after I dropped her off," Drew explained.

Mrs. Goodman waved her hand, "I don't think so. I'll drop y'all off."

"Oh, really, Mrs. Goodman. We're just down the road."

"Then all the easier." Mrs. Goodman nodded definitively, leaving no room for debate. "Miranda," she turned to her daughter. "Get my purse and get Maddy in the car."

Miranda nodded obediently and turned back to go in the house. Drew and Panda watched powerlessly, still straddling his bike, as Mrs. Goodman walked toward the garage. She entered the passcode and the door slowly rolled up. He saw Maddy and Miranda climbing into the silver minivan as the door fully came up. While Mrs. Goodman packed Evie's bike in the trunk, he strapped his little sister into the backseat.

"I'll follow you." Mrs. Goodman gave him a wide smile.

Drew nodded, giving her a tight, closed-lip smile. He felt self-conscious as he led the minivan to his house on his bike, knowing Miranda was in the front seat watching him. He was leading her to his house! *"Don't think about that,"* Panda tried to soothe. *"Evie had a great time. And now Mrs. Goodman can meet Mom. No argument any time we want to go over!"*

Drew's chest started to relax at Panda's logic. On this rare occasion, he actually agreed with Panda. He was thankful Evie had a good time. And for a fleeting moment, he was having a good time, too.

CHAPTER EIGHT

The week carried on like normal. Celeste was missing in action. Liam was being his usual revolting, phony self. Drew felt the tireless paranoia to keep Evie away from him at all times. Panda carried on with his routine disparaging comments. Drew tried not to fall asleep in class and resisted the urge to stab people with his pencil out of sheer annoyance. Sydney lounged all over Trey like a tacky fur scarf. Trey was his typical optimistic self that kept Drew from the edge of his despair. Wynter continued to make Drew feel a part of the group as he hurriedly copied her notes from first period during lunch.

All terribly monotonous.

Except for when Drew went off to the library for the last twenty minutes of lunch.

That Monday, Miranda had found him in the computer area and sat with him. She'd finished her portion of the research for their Econ project already. Drew suspected she finished it all over the weekend. "I just want to keep you company…if you don't mind," she told him behind pink cheeks. Of course, Panda didn't mind. And, timidly, Drew didn't mind very much either. Unfortunately, that meant he got the bare minimum of his research done with this new distraction.

He could care less, honestly. He already had a B in the class, and doing the minimum on the assignment wouldn't be enough to tank his grade. "*Yes, rationalize blowing off homework to hang out with Miranda,*" Panda critiqued the next time it happened. Drew had started to look forward to those precious minutes in the library. He mostly listened to Miranda as she talked about school, their project, and her plans for summer. Drew didn't mind listening. It meant he didn't have to share anything about himself. Panda worked to memorize how her eyes lit up as she talked about something she enjoyed and the way her nose scrunched up when he managed to make her laugh.

Drew found out on Tuesday that she loved to paint. Her cheeks seemed permanently pink when he finally put the pieces together that the paintings in her room were her originals. He should've guessed it sooner. Drew couldn't recall meeting someone with such talent before.

His parents didn't have any hobbies. He could care less about Liam's interests. Evie was happy to try anything at least once. Trey's talent was football. Wynter absorbed any book she could get her hands on. Drew's talent was lying to his mom and himself about being a better person for Evie. Nothing at all like what Miranda could do.

He listened intensely as she explained the craft. Right now, she was using acrylic, but she wanted to experiment with oils. Apparently, she thought of herself too much of a perfectionist to just roll with the murky edges of oils. *"Whatever all that means. She is an amazing artist!"* Even Panda was impressed, but his ego felt a little bruised. Drew and Panda lacked something that they could truly enjoy, where they could turn their brain off and create something from nothing. Drew laughed with Miranda as they related to having a little sister, and reflected concern as she spoke about her overbearing mother and her absent father. Her dad fulfilled his parenting obligation by paying his child support on time. That was the extent of her father/daughter time.

Drew was surprised and Panda showed overwhelming

excitement when she told them she had seventh period off, too. Drew had never noticed. How could he when he was always gone to pick up Evie. Miranda normally stayed at school to work on homework or study while she waited for her mom to pick her up.

That Wednesday, Miranda started walking with Drew to Howard Elementary to pick up Evie and Maddy.

On Thursday, as Evie and Maddy skipped down the sidewalk a few feet ahead of them, Miranda practically screamed, "How can you even watch football?" Drew looked back at her with wide eyes.

"It's too long for a lot of standing around. Something that is way more exciting is basketball!" She proclaimed with finality.

"*AND she watches basketball!!!*" Panda was falling for her by the minute. But Drew still felt apprehensive with Wynter's concerns in the back of his mind. Was he really committing friendship treason? He and Miranda were hanging out now more than just working on the project like Drew expected. Would Wynter be ok with it?

"*Are YOU ok with it?*" Panda gently asked him.

Drew ignored Panda's question. "I can't remember the last time I watched basketball," he said with a choked chuckle. "*It was with Dad,*" Panda painfully reminded him.

She gasped dramatically and playfully shoved him. "It's the playoffs right now! You could watch it over the weekend. Or you could come over and watch a game with me."

Panda wheezed at her suggestion. Drew shrugged. "Right, besides my last push to study for finals and our project this weekend…that leaves plenty of time to watch TV." He rolled his eyes as he awkwardly dismissed the idea. "*There's not enough time!*" Panda whined.

"Did you have to volunteer for us to go first?" Panda blurted out from behind him.

Miranda's slight giggle sent shivers down his spine, collecting in his stomach. "Always go first if you can. One," she counted, her white nail polish catching Drew's attention, "it's over with. No more nerves. Two, the teacher will be more lenient with us if we go first. Three, the teacher will actually let us do other work so long as we're not disturbing the other presentations. More study time for you."

She bumped her arm into his. The sudden contact nearly caused his feet to tangle. He drove embarrassed eyes down into the pavement. The spot on his arm she touched was now ablaze.

Panda stared at her with disbelief. "How do you know all

this?" Drew asked with skepticism, his eyes following the cracks on the sidewalk. She only offered a knowing smile. When they got back to Miranda's house, Miranda, Drew, Evie and Maddy set up shop at the dining room table. With everyone working on homework, Mrs. Goodman set out snacks. She always provided a healthy assortment of fruits or vegetables paired with cheese or crackers.

Evie was in heaven. Panda was suddenly miserable, and reminded Drew of just how opposite their house was to Miranda's. A heavy, black cloud lived over their dining room table. Drew didn't feel safe in his own home. It felt like an endless battle for existence with an inability to be himself in what should be a safe haven. It didn't use to be like that. Drew couldn't pinpoint exactly when the change happened. With him? That day during spring break? Or when his dad...?

But this...this is what their life could've been like. A warm home with natural light flowing through. A mom who was there. Granted, per Miranda, Mrs. Goodman was TOO much. But that sounded a whole lot better than what Drew and Evie had.

By the time Friday afternoon came around, Miranda and Drew had finished doing their research and put their presentation together. Miranda divided up the PowerPoint. Drew would present slides 5 through 9. She would handle the intro, slides 1 through 4, and the conclusion. Even though the project that brought them together was finished, Drew wasn't ready to go their separate ways…just yet. He was curious to explore this new friendship with someone who didn't know all of his baggage.

Drew still wanted to spend Saturday with her. And Panda didn't detect any objections from Miranda when he asked.

At home the next day, Drew asked his mom, "Are you sure you'll be here all day?" Drew needed to be certain.

"Well, we probably won't be here all day," Celeste smiled over to Evie who excitedly bit into her grilled cheese sandwich. Her smile dropped when she looked back to her son. She realized that she hadn't been explicit in her answer. "But I've got the day off. A catastrophe would have to happen." She tried to give Drew a reassuring smile.

He didn't take it.

"Call me if a catastrophe happens," Panda said out loud as Drew grabbed his bag, kissed his sister on the cheek, and headed out the door.

He pedaled to Miranda's as Panda skateboarded in circles around him. "*What are we gonna do, Romeo? Have you even thought that far ahead? Do you think maybe we were a bit harsh to Mom? Why are we still hanging out with Miranda? You said just until the project was over.*"

Drew shrugged. His nerves were mounting the more Panda talked. He decided to just focus on his immediate issue, maybe to quiet Panda a bit. "Hang out, ya know. Study?"

"*SNORE! Plus…you left your homework at home, remember? All that's in your bag is your illegal drugs. Are you hoping to sell some while wooing the girl of your dreams? Yeah, I'm sure a drug dealer is exactly her type.*"

"A movie?"

"*Too intimate.*"

"We could get a bite?"

"*And have her see us put food in our mouth?!*"

Drew groaned, "Then do you have any suggestions?"

"*Nope.*" Panda popped the P obnoxiously.

"Then keep your mouth shut." Drew leaned his bike carefully against the porch rails at Miranda's house. The flowers Evie loved were at the front of his mind. After he knocked on the door, he waited patiently. Panda chewed the inside of his cheek, shooting angry daggers at Drew. Drew refused to let Panda ruin this day. When was the last time he had time to himself? To do what he wanted?

The door swung inward. A flood of AC stung Drew's eyes. He gave a breathy grin when he saw who was on the other side of the door. Miranda didn't give him a chance to enter as she crossed the threshold, closing the front door behind her.

"Hi," her teeth were clenched in a nervous smile.

"Hi."

The pair stood for a moment. A slight breeze ruffled her dark blue dress at the knees. Drew's grip on his backpack strap caused his hand to sweat.

"Do you wanna…" Drew started. Her bright golden eyes made him falter, but Panda's unrelenting pushing encouraged him to continue, "just, cruise around on our bikes?"

She tried to bite back her smile. Drew wished she hadn't held it back. She looked down at her dress. "I have to go change."

He bit the corner of his mouth, nodding as his eyes drifted down her slim legs to his feet.

She gave an anxious "ok" before retreating inside. It was the fastest wardrobe change Drew had ever experienced. The sound of the garage opening stirred his curiosity. He wheeled his bike over as the large rolling door drew up.

Tucked neatly in the back corner, trying to hide their potential, were a paint-covered easel and a small desk that housed several paints, brushes, and cups of water. Drew figured Mrs. Goodman wouldn't risk having an errant splotch of paint on her perfect carpet.

Drew's attention wandered back to Miranda as she wheeled her bike out in front of him. Don't get him wrong, he loved seeing Miranda in dresses. But there was something just as attractive seeing her in regular clothes. As they took off down the street, Panda kept trying to point out how much her shorts had ridden up her thigh as she pedaled. Or how the breeze pulled back on her baggy shirt, the front tucked into her waistband.

Panda's imagination started to run amuck. *"Imagine pulling that shirt out and…"*

"Stop it!" Drew inwardly snapped at Panda.

And to Drew's surprise, Panda remained quiet.

For a while Miranda and Drew just cruised around the neighborhood, enjoying the warm May sun and the gentle breeze. They eventually stopped at the playground at Howard Elementary. Miranda raced him to the swing set and won. He tossed his bag down by the pole and felt the sun beat down on his black pant legs. It was times like this when he wished Panda didn't cut him. He only had five on his calves, but it was obvious what the scars were. It was enough to make him feel shame and require him to hide his mutilation.

"Can I ask you a personal question?" Drew asked, his heart was starting to hammer. Maybe this was a bad idea. He looked to Panda for help. "*There are worse questions I could ask if you want! Like the rumor she started about Wynter. OR about her dad!*"

"Is that the game we're playing now?" Miranda focused on her feet that were slightly dangling off the ground. She drifted slightly.

"You don't have to…"

She snickered to herself. "Come on. Don't chicken out on me now."

"Why do you hang out with Sydney Porter? She's not exactly the nicest girl in school."

"And I am?" Miranda's doubtful eyes made Drew's heart jump to his throat. She shrugged and looked back down at the ground. "She was nice to me. She saw me when no one else did."

"*I saw you!*" Panda yelled. Drew's chest thumped trying to keep him quiet.

"Is it my turn now?" She grinned.

"Your turn?"

"We are playing the personal questions game, right?" She raised a challenging brow at him.

He turned his mouth down in agreeance. "Bet. Go ahead."

"Can you explain why your uncle is living with you?" She looked at him with apprehension. When Drew didn't answer, her neck strained in panic. "I'm sorry. It's none of my business."

Drew released a heavy sigh. "It's ok." He kept his eyes trained on the wood chips beneath him, trying to find words to explain his weird family dynamic. Only Trey and Wynter knew the real reason. Everyone else had fun spreading rumors around school. Half-baked, disgusting, semi-truths. *What if Miranda knows about those rumors?*

"Have you heard anything at school?" Panda asked suspiciously.

She bobbed her head side to side. "I wanted to hear the truth from you."

"Are you sure about this?" Panda warned. Drew took a deep breath, finding his courage. "When my dad died, my uncle thought my mom needed help around the house. She really

didn't argue with him." His brows bunched together in irritation. "And I guess his income does help her pay bills but…"

"But you still feel like you do everything?" Miranda finished for him softly.

Drew finally looked at her. Her eyes were sad, but also kind and comforting. "When did your dad die?"

"Last year," Drew muttered out. His throat felt thick.

"I'm sorry." She reached her hand out and touched his arm. Drew didn't move. He wasn't sure what to do now. "What happened to him? If you don't mind…"

"You know, we've skipped your turn…like twice?" Drew tried to disguise his vulnerability with humor. Miranda dropped her hand to her lap, forcing a smile at his joke.

Drew's eyes flicked to Panda. The furry beast seemed just as lost. No one ever asked him point-blank what happened. His stomach flipped as he remembered the day he found out. He was sixteen when it happened. The anniversary was just a couple of months ago. His chest squeezed. His grip on the swing set tightened. Not even Panda could stop the oncoming memory…

His mom had pulled Drew and Evie out of school early that day. Celeste's cheeks had dried tear tracks down her face. Her face looked sunken in. Her gaze was far away as she gripped the steering wheel, trying to get them home. She didn't hear Drew's concern as he asked her what was wrong for the second time. Evie kept looking to Drew for answers. Her wide brown eyes were terrified. He reached over and held her hand the whole ride home.

Once inside the house, Celeste sat them down on the couch. She crouched in front of them and held both their hands in a tight grip. She looked like she was going to start crying again.

"Mommy, what's wrong?" Evie asked first.

Celeste licked her lips. She blinked furiously, unsure of how to get the words out. "I talked to Daddy's boss, sweetheart."

"What's wrong?" Drew asked in a stiff voice. His heart dropped to his stomach at the weight of his mom's behavior.

She looked between her two children. Fear and sorrow seemed submerged in her eyes. She licked her lips and tried again, "Daddy got really hurt." Evie sat there, not quite understanding what happened to their father. "He's not coming home."

"He died!" Drew yelled at his mom, not meaning to raise his voice.

Celeste closed her eyes. She flinched as if she was electro-cuted by his response. Her tears started again. Drew pulled away, stood up and started pacing the living room. He didn't hear his mom whispering to Evie, trying to explain what had happened using words she would understand. Everything around him seemed to fade away. He couldn't breathe right. He couldn't stop shaking. He was afraid that if he'd stopped his pacing, he would crumble to the ground. Evie's howling sobs leaked through his ears. Celeste clutched her tightly.

Then, there had been a knock at the front door. With Evie wrapped around their mom in a tense koala hold, Celeste had opened the door. His uncle stood there panting. As if he'd ran over instead of driving there.

"I got here as soon as I could," Liam said as he came inside. Evie screamed louder when she saw their father's twin, having a hard time understanding that it was Liam and not their dad. Liam held his mom and sister in a strong hug. Drew gazed at his broken family and felt hollow. There he was, left on the outskirts of his own family on the second worst day of his life.

Drew looked over to Miranda's patient waiting eyes as the memory finished reeling through his mind. He felt his chest constrict and looked up toward the sun. Squeezing his eyes closed, he resisted the burning need to cry. "*It's ok.*" Panda sympathized. "*Dad's story should be shared.*"

"He uh…" Drew's voice came out raspy. Clearing his throat, he started again. "My dad was in the Army. Overseas. I can't remember the name of the country." He shook his head. "My mom told me his unit was trying to return to their base. But there was an ambush. My dad managed to warn the other surrounding units what was happening." Drew pinched his nose closed and then sniffed hard. He blinked rapidly to clear his vision. "He saved twenty people with his warning. But his unit didn't make it."

Drew's heart pounded as sweat pooled on his hands. He couldn't bear to see the look on Miranda's face. Clearing his throat loudly, he started kicking his legs under him. He gripped the metal chain on the swing set so hard he could feel the metal digging into his flesh. He gained more momentum. Miranda followed suit. She knew that he'd reached his maximum sharing capacity. As they swung back and forth, he thankfully let her change the subject and do the talking for them both.

After about thirty minutes, Drew's breathing started to return to normal. His hard exterior was beginning to soften again as they gently moved their swings next to each other.

Suddenly, the loud ringtone on his phone interrupted Miranda mid-sentence. He clumsily dug around his pocket, careful his phone didn't take a nosedive into the wood chips. His eyes slanted when he saw the name of the caller. Panda groaned in irritation.

"What?" Drew rumbled.

Miranda sucked in a sudden breath as Drew immediately stood up. His chest compressed. His legs buzzed. Panda began to hyperventilate.

"Who's with Evie?" Panda gasped for air. Miranda stared at his rigid back with worry. "I'm on my way." Drew didn't wait for a reply before disconnecting the call. He ran to his bike, forgetting his backpack by the pole.

"Drew?" Miranda hopped off the swing. She ignored the scrape on her thighs as the rough plastic pulled on her skin.

"I'm sorry Miranda," Drew called over his shoulder as he mounted his bike. "I've got to go!"

CHAPTER NINE

Drew had never pedaled so fast in his life. "*Faster! Must go FASTER!*" Panda ordered. Drew's bike tires screeched to a halt on his front lawn. He jumped off as the frame toppled to the side. What little grass they had was easily covered by his bike. Out of breath, Drew barged into the house.

"Evie!"

With jelly legs still pushing him forward, he entered deeper. "*What if we're too late?*" His heart beat wildly in his chest. His lungs screamed for more oxygen. His t-shirt clung to him with sweat.

"Evie!" Drew shouted louder with Panda's help projecting his voice.

Drew nearly collided into Evie as she rounded the

corner, smiling from ear to ear. She ran up to him and threw her arms around his waist. Drew froze for a moment in shock before he could fully inhale the oxygen his lungs desperately needed. It was like his brain released a floodgate of blood throughout the rest of his body, calming his nerves. He gasped and held her strongly. But it wasn't enough. He had to be sure she was ok. He picked her up and held her close.

"Are you ok?"

She bobbed her head wildly. "Uncle Liam and I are making spaghetti. Wanna help?"

Then, Uncle Liam joined them in the hallway. Drew took a step back and pressed Evie closer to his chest protectively. "Hey dude," Liam's smug smirk made Panda want to punch him in the face. "You got here quick. The water isn't even boiling yet."

Celeste came home after dinner. Liam cleaned the kitchen while Drew played with Evie on the floor in the living room. In a heartbeat, Evie left Drew and jumped up to hug their mom. Celeste expertly balanced Evie on her hip as she dove into the freezer for ice cream, rambling on about how one of the new residents failed to follow regulations. To no one in particular, she recounted that because it was her patient, the administrator thought she'd be the best person to smooth things over. Panda suspected the hospital just wanted to avoid a lawsuit and that the administrator wasn't doing such a swell job to calm the patient.

Drew feigned interest. Liam hung on her every word. Evie was just fixated on getting dessert. Shortly, all four of them sat at the table while the hollow scrapes of spoons in bowls droned on in Drew's ears. Drew involuntarily flinched each time Evie brutally stabbed at the frozen chocolate shell with her dull instrument. His nervous system was rattled from his panic attack earlier. *"Celeste is home now. Probably a good night to go out,"* Panda planned.

"I think that's a great idea. Drew, what do you think? Drew?"

His head snapped up. The dark thoughts he was occupied with suddenly thrust him back to the dining room. "What?"

"Did you hear Liam's suggestion?" Celeste, using her spoon, pointed to the thing sitting beside her.

Panda snorted. *"Of course not! We're not paying attention to that jerk!"* Drew just shook his head no.

"I was telling your mom," Liam arrogantly repeated, "that I thought you should spend the summer at my shop."

"I think it'd be great," Celeste smiled tenderly.

"You'd learn a thing or two about cars. Finally break that

bad habit of yours." Liam's head tilted down slightly. But his true intention shone through as he looked at Drew past his furry brows.

Celeste blinked back and forth between the two of them. Her brow creased as she initially missed the underlying point of Liam's jab. "What?" she asked, confused at first. But her patience wore thin as she saw her son's grip on his spoon tighten. Her eyes narrowed slightly. "Drew." Her tone was demanding. Not a suggestion or a question. A command.

"I don't know what Liam is talking about," Panda answered for Drew through gritted teeth.

"What's going on, Drew?" Celeste raised her voice. Drew saw Evie shrink back into her chair at their mom's sharp voice.

Liam interrupted his mother with his big brother act. "Can we not, dude? I saw your backpack last week."

"You knew and you didn't tell me?!" Celeste accused, flashing betrayed eyes to Liam. Looking back to her son, "Are you selling drugs again?" Her voice went up an octave. Her eyes wild with anger.

"What are you doing snooping around in my bag for?" Panda snapped, yelling at his uncle.

"Drew!" His mom demanded. "I thought we were done

with all of this! Did you even stop? Did you not learn from this?"

Celeste kept yelling while Liam stared at Drew. Panda was very aware of how Evie was watching the three of them. Her ice cream, forgotten, started to turn soupy. Condensation dripped from the chocolate shell. It looked like an iceberg floating in a sea of vanilla.

"Why are you all yelling?!" Evie burst out, her eyes watery with concern. Drew watched in disgust as his uncle impatiently rolled his eyes. Celeste turned toward Evie, trying to calm her. Drew wanted to console his little sister, but Liam was his first priority at the moment.

"I don't know what you THINK you saw, Liam," Drew tried to relax his posture. "But there wasn't anything in my bag except homework."

"Prove it." Liam challenged.

"Go get me your bag right now!" Celeste ordered, snapping her fingers toward the stairwell to the basement.

"*Oh shit...*"

"Fine." Drew growled at his uncle.

Too wrapped up in anger and pettiness, Drew dramatically threw his spoon into his bowl, causing a loud ringing of ceramic to echo throughout the room that mixed with

Evie's haggard sobs. He scraped his chair against the hardwood floor as he stood up. The screeching made Evie wince. He stalked down the stairs. Panda decided that he would replay the look on Evie's face to haunt Drew later but he couldn't focus on that right now. Where was his backpack?

"Fuck! You left it at the park!" Panda's hands flew into his hair. *"Omar is going to kill us if we don't get his shit back!"*

"Oh shit," Drew gasped. "We'll have to fix that later! One problem at a time." He hurriedly dove into his closet for a spare backpack. His bag from last year. He had nearly a dozen, discarded backpacks. His mom always had to buy him a new one for the start of the school year because he and Panda were so rough with them. For once, Panda being a pack rat had actually come in handy. The problem with last year's bag was that the zippers were stuck on two of the three pockets. He quickly shoved his notebooks and text-books inside the main compartment. Homework ripped and crinkled with his quick movements.

He jolted out of his skin as Celeste and Liam barged into his room. The smack of the door against the wall made Drew's heart jump up to his throat.

"I was coming back upstairs," Drew managed to mutter

out past his clenched jaw.

"Just had to make sure you weren't hiding anything." Liam's eyes wandered around Drew's messy room, the judgment prevalent on his pretentious face. Celeste snatched Drew's bag out of his hands. She struggled with the two broken zippers. In frustration, she dumped the contents of his bag out. Textbooks clashed to the floor, threatening to break their spines. Homework ripped and tore even more. Drew felt the chasm between him and his mom grow wider.

"That's not the bag you had last week," Liam accused.

"It broke," Panda's back teeth clenched with rage at Liam. Drew's heart was in pieces at his mom. They both were shocked at how the evening turned out.

Celeste exhaled heavily once the bag was empty. "Another bag, Drew?"

"No point in making a big deal about it. I've got a week left of school."

"Drew," his mom sighed tiredly. She was spent. "*It must be a burden to have you as her child,*" Panda echoed Drew's thoughts. Celeste's voice was pleading, trying to reach across the wide sea between them. "I can't go through it again."

The start of last summer had been eventful. The cops

brought Drew home after a house party got raided. It wasn't Trey's, thank goodness. But that was beside the point. Normally, Drew hated pity. But he graciously took the judge's pity on him, considering he was a minor and it was his first offense. "This is your only warning," he remembered the judge threatened. Doing community service wasn't the best way to spend his summer, but it was better than serving time. It nearly broke Celeste and things only got worse for Drew when Liam moved in a few weeks after that. "*It's your fault Liam moved in,*" Panda blamed. "*It makes protecting and providing for Evie that much harder.*"

Drew didn't think he had much of a choice until now. But he was too scared to tell Omar he quit. Besides, it was good, easy money. At the time, it was anyways. Now, it wasn't worth the double life it was costing him. "*We can't go to jail! We'll find our own way. Not through Omar and not Liam. Evie deserves better than a drug dealer for a brother,*" Panda insisted.

"Drew?" Celeste tried again. "Tell me the truth. I won't have a repeat of last summer!"

"I'm not dealing drugs, Mom," Drew answered delicately. "Not since last year."

Celeste took a visible, shaky breath. "Ok." She gently handed him back his battered backpack. Panda snatched it from her hand.

She breathed in sharply. "I'm sorry," she apologized with her back straight. But her limbs looked so tired. Her eyes glared at Liam as she turned and left Drew's room before heading back up the stairs to care for Evie. Liam stared Drew down.

"You going to toss my room?" Drew antagonized. "By all means, you won't find anything."

Liam looked around, as if seriously contemplating going through Drew's things. "Get out," Panda snarled when his uncle didn't answer.

Liam huffed, his face twisting into a condescending sneer. He turned and exited as Drew requested. Drew slammed his door closed behind him and sank on the floor. His nails raked over his dry curls. Panda paced around the room and started to panic. "*We have to find our bag! Do you think by some miracle it's still at the park? Shit! What if it's gone? How the hell do we explain that to Omar?*"

"We're done," Drew exhaled. His head was swimming.

"*You're damn right we're done if Omar finds out! We're cooked!*" Panda rattled.

"No, I mean, we're done with this whole mess! I'm sick of dealing with Omar, sick of Liam, and sick of making Mom feel like shit."

"*Fine, whatever,*" Panda dismissed. "*I can't believe you lost the bag! Omar is going to hunt us down and kill us! He's going to come to our house. Murder our whole family in front of us, make us watch, and then kill us.*"

Drew's heart rate picked up. Panda was right. Omar knew exactly where he was. If they didn't get that bag back…Drew's face paled at the thought.

"We have to find my backpack," Drew whispered.

"*Miranda!*" Panda snapped his fingers as the idea popped in Drew's head.

Following Panda's train of thought, Drew whipped his phone out and paused. There was an unread text from Miranda. He and Panda released heavy sighs of relief.

MIRANDA: FYI I've got your backpack.

How did he not notice this? She sent it nearly three hours ago! Almost as soon as he bailed on her. It seemed that his panic attack and watching Evie had consumed him. He texted her back with fury.

DREW: Thank you! Can I swing by and grab it?

He only had to wait a second.

MIRANDA: Of course. Whenever.

Drew picked himself up, straightened his clothes, turned

his light out, and stormed upstairs. He headed toward the back door.

"Where you headed?" Celeste called from the couch. His eye twitched before he turned toward the living room. The glow of the TV bathed Celeste and Evie in blue. He was thankful Liam wasn't there with them. Drew didn't care enough to ask where he went.

"Out," Panda said firmly. Celeste didn't argue. She thought he was still angry and needed to blow off some steam for being falsely accused. Drew wasn't going to correct her.

His bike was where he left it. He was surprised Liam and Celeste didn't grill him for leaving his bike out front.

"*Dude!*" Panda snapped at him. "*What if Miranda looked in it?*" Drew's stomach sank at the thought. "*She'll definitely look at us differently. No one wants to date such a loser! You don't think she took any, do you? To impress Porter or the other jocks in that stupid clique?*" Panda's spinning thoughts overwhelmed Drew with infinite what-ifs. He couldn't help replaying the sickly incident in his mind.

Adrenaline pumped through Drew's veins as he pedaled his bike. Dusk turned into evening and the calm night did wonders for his nerves. The sky settled into a dark blue. The streetlights glowed a warm, blurred, mustard yellow as the asphalt turned a shiny purple from the light evening drizzle. Drew breathed in the smell of damp grass. Fresh rain always made him feel clean, unsoiled for a moment, like the terrible, heinous shit in his life never happened.

"Yeah…for a moment."

Drew ignored Panda's snide comment. He focused on absorbing the cool air, feeling it flood his bloodstream. It was like his whole system restored itself to baseline. He didn't even realize that it was still drizzling because his skin was so on fire. By the time he made it to Miranda's, the top of his shirt was wet.

An older smile greeted him. "Drew! Come on in darlin'."

"Thanks, Mrs. Goodman." Drew ducked inside, a little breathless. The AC raised goosebumps along his damp skin. He was suddenly aware of his wet shirt as it weighed heavily on his shoulders.

"What brings you by?" She held her large purple robe tightly against her. She didn't look at all ready for bed though. She still had her makeup on. Drew detected jeans still wrapped around her bamboo thin legs. *"If she's cold, maybe she could turn off the freaking AC!"* Panda shivered beside him.

"Sorry to bother you, but Miranda's expecting me. I left

my bag by mistake."

"Oh," Mrs. Goodman blinked in surprise. "No problem. She's in her room. Go on ahead."

Panda's eyes widened in shock. "Really?"

"Yeah, she's up there." The sound on the TV caused Mrs. Goodman's ears to perk up. She quickly dashed over to the living room, like a moth drawn to bright light.

"Ok, thanks." Drew kicked off his wet shoes and then tiptoed up the freshly vacuumed stairs.

He paused outside Miranda's bedroom. The light leaked out the bottom of the closed door, bathing his feet in possibility. Otherwise, the hallway was completely dark. He heard music on the other side. "*Get closer. What's she listening to?*" Drew didn't recognize the song. But it sounded peaceful, gentle. Sad even. Lo-fi maybe? With a deep breath, he knocked on the door.

"Come in!"

Drew flinched at the innocent request. He knocked on the door again. "It's…uh…it's me." His voice sounded grave with hesitation.

The music almost became inaudible. The door opened quickly. He flinched again from the sudden motion and squinted from the light. Drew's eyes swiftly recovered as his eyes took in Miranda. Her chocolate waves pooled over her shoulders, and her tank top sported bare arms, spelling out PINK in large letters across her round chest. His eyes followed down her tight abdomen to the short—"*Very short!*" Panda exclaimed—black shorts she wore. Her muscular, athletic legs were on full display for him.

Drew snapped his eyes back to her startled, chocolate eyes. Panda drooled beside him. "*Can you tell if black people blush? Well, you're mixed. But you're definitely blushing! You've stared for way too long, bro!*" Drew tried to keep his face neutral as Panda teased him, suddenly aware of how hot his face felt.

Miranda opened the door wider and Drew accepted her silent invitation. She sealed them in her bright room once he entered and he easily found his bag on her desk chair. He went over and tentatively picked it up.

"Thanks for grabbing it," he said with his back to her.

"Is everything ok?" Miranda practically whispered. Her question hung in the air, swirling around Drew's head like a tornado. Where would he even begin?

He turned around to face her. The pained look on her face stabbed him in the chest. "Fine. Sorry for running out like that."

Her head tilted slightly. Was she giving him a chance to be honest? Open up?

"I…" she started. She looked at the floor for a moment before looking back at him. Her eyes hardened in that millisecond, "I looked inside." His spine straightened. "*I told you so!*" Panda gasped. "Is everything ok?" she asked again.

But Drew felt the radius of her concern change. Before, it was like she was asking about his well-being. Maybe asking if his family was ok. That'd be the only reasonable excuse for leaving as suddenly as he did. Now she was specifically asking about one thing: Drew's safety. If he was in any trouble. Drew always found himself in trouble. But she was asking on a criminal basis.

"I'm done."

She crossed her arms and thought about her next words. "That's not what I asked."

"I'm fine. And I'm done." He dipped his head. "*Well, not yet we aren't. But soon…*" Panda corrected. "You don't have to worry about me."

"That's for me to decide," Miranda spoke softly, her voice determined. Drew picked his head back up and saw that her face was screwed up with concern. Maybe anger? "Why?" she continued.

"I don't want to anymore."

"No…" she rubbed the middle of her forehead for a moment. "I mean…why did you do it in the first place?"

Drew tried to avoid her probing gaze. But everywhere he looked, there was Miranda, or a part of her, staring back at him. The pictures on her vanity. Her paintings that threatened to suck him in and leave him desolate in that immense forest. He shrugged, "I needed something else for a while to distract me. I got swept up in all of it." He continued, trying to put his actions into words, "I convinced myself for a while that I was helping my mom. Buying groceries a few times. Buying clothes and toys for Evie. Buying my own stuff whenever I needed it. Then I got busted last year. Lied and told my mom I quit."

"But you didn't?" Miranda's tone seemed to turn harsh as she tried to follow his disjointed confession.

"No…" Drew ran a tired hand across his head, his palm still slick with rainwater. "It all just turned into feeling good at something. Money I could spend on Evie. Invest in myself. Spend on things I wanted."

"So…why stop now?"

Drew looked down at her. Her features were rigid, but smooth like marble, save for the worry line between her brows. "*A line you are causing!*" Panda blamed. "Because of Evie," he said softly.

"You did it for Evie?" Miranda asked in disbelief.

Drew nodded.

She rubbed her temples in confusion. "So, you started for Evie and now you're stopping for her?" Drew nodded again. "You do realize how contradicting that sounds right?"

"I know."

"Do you? Dealing drugs is not helping her, Drew. It doesn't help anyone if you get in trouble." He'd heard this same speech from Trey and Wynter. But now, he was hearing it from Miranda, someone who barely knew Drew's history like his friends did. It just hit different. "I get it. I really do. But don't ever bring that shit to my house again," Miranda finished.

Drew stiffened hearing her swear. Her face was hard with finality, but her eyes were watery.

Oh God, do I scare her? Drew didn't want that for her. He didn't want to make anyone feel that way. But he did, didn't he? How many times had Wynter told him the same thing? How worried was Trey for him? There was the jumbled pool of emotions from his mom. Evie had even witnessed a few of the transactions. Right in front of her!

"*You've got to be the worst person on the planet,*" Panda chimed in.

CHAPTER TEN

Drew blissfully replayed the last moment with Miranda on a loop in his mind the entire time he biked to Omar's apartment. Miranda had hugged him. "*She hugged us!!!!*" Panda exploded with delight. He was captivated by how much clarity he had. For a moment, Drew had just stood there like a dope until Panda helped him bring his arms up around her back. Once he did that, it was like Miranda fell into him deeper. He placed his cheek on top of her head, marveling at how soft her hair felt. She really did smell like strawberries. Her arms wrapped tightly around his slim waist, begging him to remain anchored there for a moment longer.

God, how he wished he could've stayed there longer. When Drew knocked on Omar's door, the blaring TV inside the apartment died down. He looked around, a bit uneasy on the rickety, metal walkway, and stuffed his hands in his pockets. His backpack was becoming heavier by the minute. He'd chained his bike to the railing of the stairs. In a neighborhood like this though, a simple bike lock wasn't much of a deterrent.

It was Drew's second time being at Omar's apartment. The first was when Omar brought Drew onboard. The deal was that Drew would sell Omar's drugs and bring him money regularly from the sales. If he kept up the deal, Drew could keep 5 percent of the cash for himself. If he crossed Omar, then Drew's life would be in danger. *"Probably beat to a pulp! Or worse!"* Panda reminded Drew. Normally, they met at a place Omar approved of—usually the park—for the money and drug exchanges, so Drew was nervous that he had showed up unannounced at Omar's door.

The strong smell of weed punched Drew in the nose as the door suddenly opened inward. Omar thrust his head out the door. His long dreadlocks swayed left and right as he inspected the walkway. Peering around Drew, Omar looked for any bystanders.

"What the fuck are you doing here?" Omar accused.

"I…I…" Drew stammered. *"We should've texted him first!"*

Panda shuddered with fear. "…I'm sorry, man, I had to talk to you. It's kind of an emergency." Omar's long, skinny fingers wrapped around Drew's shirt in a tight grip, then pulled him stumbling inside the hazy apartment. Omar slammed the door closed and locked the deadbolt, then put the chain lock in place. Drew stood still as he waited for permission to talk, to move, *"to breathe!"* Panda gulped.

The whole apartment felt filmy and smelled like Drew's gym sweatpants after they had stewed in his locker over the weekend. He glanced down at the immensely dirty floor compared to Miranda's, and then over to the dishes piled in the small kitchen sink. Open pizza boxes were snuggled between bongs on the coffee table. Drew's heart raced when he spotted Jay, Omar's cousin, *"and muscle,"* Panda reminded, on the couch, like the fat blueberry he was. Jay grunted in acknowledgement to Drew. Drew dipped his chin down in response.

A woman he didn't know with long pink braids claimed a chair all to herself. Her legs draped over the arm of the small chair, her focus on the TV. Images of Cowboys on horses kicking up dirt as they rode across a desert had her undivided attention.

Omar wore an undershirt that was tucked inside his

oversized jeans. Satisfied with the apartment's security, he pulled on a cigarette Drew didn't notice he was holding on to. Omar turned to face Drew, his face angrily twisted. "You know better than to show up like this!" He blew smoke in Drew's face and tapped his middle finger harshly on Drew's chest while he pinched the cigarette between his forefinger and thumb. Drew fought to keep his face neutral as more smoke clawed up his nose.

Omar slowly stalked toward the couch. "This better be good." He sat down beside his cousin and propped a dirty shoe a little too close to the open pizza box for Drew's comfort. Drew perched himself on the edge of the only other available chair adjacent to the couch. The gaudy flowers on the upholstery reminded him of his grandma's furniture. Panda stood stiff as a board behind him.

"Sorry for dropping by like this Omar…"

"What do you want, Drew?" Omar moved his cigarette to his mouth, sounding more tired than irritable now. "You need more?" he asked in disbelief.

"No, I actually…" Drew pulled his hands out of his pockets and wiped them on his jeans. His eyes drifted to the glassy gaze of Jay. He looked slow and inebriated. But Drew and Panda also once saw Jay slap someone unconscious.

Drew wasn't looking to leave Omar's apartment a bruised, bloody mess. "…I want out, man."

Omar released more smoke toward the ceiling. "Out? What 'cha mean, OUT?" His narrow eyes slanted even more in growing anger. "That motherfucker Wallace didn't get to you, did he?" He pointed a slim finger to the left.

"Nah, Omar…" Drew shook his head. A shadow shifted in the hallway, causing Drew to halt. He watched a small, plump child in a diaper and shirt that barely stretched over his rolls make a beeline for the pizza.

Omar stretched a long leg over toward Drew. The impromptu gate stopped the child. "Nat!" he barked at the young woman on the chair. Her head lazily rolled toward him. "Get him outta here!"

With her attention still on the TV, she sucked on her teeth and replied, "You take care of him. I've taken care of those damn kids all day."

Drew watched the exchange with a stone in his stomach. Panda cringed, *"We really caught him on a bad day."* The boy was starting to get fussy as he pushed against Omar's leg. Jay remained immobile as he continued to stare off into space.

"Bitch," Omar called back to her. "Can't you see I'm fucking busy here trying to handle business? Get your lazy ass up and take care of this for me."

She groaned and rolled off the chair, snatching up the small child with her long, manicured talon-like nails, and disappeared into the back room. Drew heard muffled fussing behind the closed door.

Omar dropped his leg and leaned forward. He tapped his cigarette on an ashtray and then leaned back, "Continue."

Drew kept staring down the hall. His concern suddenly shifted to the kid and he wondered if there were any other children there. Panda smacked him upside the head. *"Evie first before snitching to CPS."*

"No lie," Drew managed to find his words again. "I'm not working with Wallace or anyone else, Omar."

Omar just stared at him.

Drew knew he was waiting for a better explanation. "My mom almost busted me tonight. I can't get in trouble again. Ya know. I've got my little sister to take care of."

"What?" Jay wheezed out. "Scared of going to jail?"

"No," Panda answered sternly. "But I've got a little sister. She needs me," Drew finished before Panda could say anymore.

"You got a daddy and a mommy, don't you?" Jay suddenly came to life and his stout knuckles tightened a bit. Drew wasn't sure if Jay wanted to take a swing at him or take another hit off the bong. Panda prayed for the latter.

"Nah, man…" Omar interjected, his leg bounced once, twice on the table. "His daddy's a war hero." He looked back to Drew. With mock sympathy, he corrected his statement. "My bad, man, WAS a war hero. Mom's a baddie down at the hospital. Say…" he snapped his fingers at Drew in recollection, "…isn't your uncle living with you?" Omar squinted at Drew. "Word on the street is he's getting awfully friendly with your mom."

Jay snickered, "Sounds like sloppy seconds compared to a war hero."

Omar and Jay laughed at Drew.

"That's gotta be weird, right?" Omar continued. "I heard he's your daddy's twin."

"Do you think yo' momma is comparin' them?" Jay laughed, his gap-toothed mouth on full display.

"Or," Omar jabbed Jay in the side, "maybe she pretends it's still his daddy." The two cracked up like it was the greatest joke on the planet.

"Are you gonna let them talk to you like this? Punch that asshole in the face!" Panda steamed. Drew's fists tightened. He felt like he was going to snap. He wanted to yell and punch Omar

like Panda suggested. He'd heard those same disgusting rumors at school. Instead of lashing out, Drew took slow, even breaths.

Omar's laughter died down. He eyed Drew carefully. His cruel smile disappeared and his eyes narrowed as he debated whether or not he should goad Drew some more. Instead, he took a long drag of his cigarette. "Drew, you know I can't let you go. You're my best pusher."

"Ok, what if I sold off the rest. Or returned it to you? Then I'm out?" Drew tried to negotiate.

Omar choked on a laugh. A sluggish smile pulled his mouth up. He sat up and pressed his cigarette into the ashtray before he snatched Drew's bag out of his hand. His smile dropped as he turned his glassy eyes back to Drew. "Are you trying to boss me around in my own house?" Before Drew could argue, Omar was up and stomping around. He pulled out the money Drew had in his bag and started counting. "You're short. I'll take all this plus another fifty."

Drew hurriedly went for his wallet in his pocket to pay off the difference. "I haven't sold the rest yet."

Drew limply held out the cash, which Omar promptly snatched from his hand. "You show up at my house, you could've been followed, then you demand to be out when you haven't gotten me the rest of my fucking money?! Are you stupid?!"

Drew felt like shrinking in his seat but stayed still. Panda observed Jay closely. To their relief, he hadn't moved. He just stared at Drew with disappointment.

Omar opened a drawer in the coffee table and started stuffing Drew's bag with more weed and baggies of pills. "Since you my best man, you should have no problem selling the rest of this, too! I know you've got that end-of-year high school party coming up. Finish this up and bring me the cash. Then we're square!"

Omar threw the now stuffed bag onto Drew's lap. Panda flinched at Omar's reaction, "*This isn't going at all like we had hoped!*" Drew tried to play it cool even though it felt like all the wind got knocked out of him. He started to nod in compliance, but stopped when Omar sneered, "And Drew," he jabbed a finger at him, "if I find out you back on these streets and God forbid, I find out you teamed up with fuckboy Wallace, ol' Jay is going to beat yo narrow black ass. Capeesh?"

Jay grunted, giving Drew half a smile, almost like he was looking forward to the impending ass whooping.

Panda audibly exhaled, "Capeesh."

CHAPTER ELEVEN

Drew stayed out all night, mostly hanging around the outside of the mall until it closed. By eleven o'clock, he managed to sell off half the new product Omar had loaded on him. A run-in with the mall's rent-a-cop sent him sprinting to the other side of the building. It wasn't that hard to outrun him, but it left Drew and Panda anxious about their surroundings and ready to bolt at any minute. He hated this.

After the mall closed, Drew biked downtown, pushing into Wallace's territory. It was Panda's brilliant idea. Omar wouldn't like this, but Drew was desperate to unload as quickly as possible. It's not like Drew was directly in Wallace's backyard and his well-known streets. He just looked for a few people going to the clubs who wanted the uppers that he could provide. A couple of his older classmates who had graduated recognized him. Because his reputation proceeded him, just like that, half the uppers were gone.

Drew snuck back into his house around three in the morning and immediately passed out. He was over the moon when Trey and Wynter said they were free to come over that Sunday afternoon and hang out. It'd felt like ages since all three of them were able to spend time together outside of school. He needed some sort of celebration. He was so close to being out. *"And we need a distraction from the fact that we only have a week left to unload the rest of our gear for Omar!"* Panda reminded him.

That Sunday, sounds of button mashing and chip crunching echoed in the room. As they sat on the futon couch, Trey bumped into Drew repeatedly, as if the motion of his body made him a better fighter in their video game. Wynter sat as far into the corner of the couch as she could, away from Trey's shoulder bumping. She lazily munched on chips while she waited to fight the winner. Panda busied himself by stuffing his face with chips, causing Drew's controller to get greasy.

Drew was so close to separating himself from Omar. He thought that if he could sell off the rest BEFORE Trey's party, it would be even better! *"Cake,"* Panda agreed. He was so done with his junior year.

They barely heard a hollow knock over the sounds of the game.

"Yeah?!" Drew craned his neck toward the door while he muttered curse words to Trey after he took half his life with a combo move.

"Hey guys. Just wanted to drop these off." Celeste entered with a fresh batch of pizza rolls.

"Thanks, Mrs. Collins," Wynter helped her set the tray down, taking in the scent of cheese and pepperoni.

"You guys staying for dinner?" Drew's mom took a step back.

"If you don't mind?" Wynter shrugged. She didn't even bother looking over at the guys.

"Uh…" Trey attempted to string a sentence together. "Maybe?"

"Boo-yah!" Drew shouted triumphantly. Trey resisted the urge to throw the controller across the room and instead tossed it to Wynter, who noticed how warm it was. Drew took a deep breath as he looked at his mom. "You're off tonight, right?"

"Yup," she crossed her arms. "I'm not even on-call. If the

building catches on fire, it's someone else's problem." She lightly chuckled.

"Can I go out then if that's the case?"

Her weary eyes creased a bit. Celeste knew he was out late last night and her knee-jerk reaction was to tell him no. She didn't even know what time he got home, a sign that he wasn't done dealing. But her heart pinched a little. Maybe he was still mad that she accused him in the first place. Maybe he simply wanted a day without responsibility.

Before she turned to go back upstairs, Celeste slowly nodded her head. Wynter helped herself to loading a new match as Drew focused on the chips. The image of Omar's dirty shoes last night was singed in his memory, turning his stomach off the small bite-sized pizza that Trey was quickly claiming.

"So…" Wynter spoke easily as their match started. "I heard back from the transfer program…"

"And?" Trey asked with a mouthful. Drew's stomach tightened at her possible answer.

Panda immediately went off the rails. *"What if she gets in?! She'll be gone for a whole year! A YEAR! She's our best friend. She can't disappear like that. Oh God, what if she doesn't miss us? What if this is the start of us growing apart? What if she doesn't get in?*

She'd be devastated. And we'd be the piece of shit who is so selfishly happy she didn't go. We're the worst."

Her smile popped, unable to resist it anymore. "I got in!" Drew paused the game. Her squealing was already enough of a disruption. Trey cheered alongside her and they all hugged each other in a frenzy. Suddenly the reality hit them. Drew's arms grew slack and Panda paused in his chewing, *"She'll never come back now."*

"Drew?"

He numbly turned his head to her. Her wild curls framed her round face. Her smoky grey eyes were wide with expectation. Why did his chest hurt so much?

He blinked his sadness away and smiled crookedly, "I guess this is our year to all go to prom, huh?" A grin stretched across her face. She threw her arms around his neck and laughed like a maniac. Panda caused butterflies to erupt in Drew's stomach as he inhaled the smell of her coconut lotion.

Trey leaned back with a satisfied smirk, "We're going out for sure now. I'll drive!" He picked up the controller and started turning the systems off.

"Grab your backpack!" Panda ordered. Drew hesitated. He was aware of the deadline he'd given himself to be done with

Omar, but he just wanted an afternoon with his friends. He wanted to act normal and focus on spending time with Trey and Wynter. "*And what if Liam decides to snoop in our room again?!*" Panda waved his arms wildly in panic. Drew's chest tightened at that possibility. While his friends waited outside for him, Drew hid his backpack under his bed, surrounded by clothes. It was a good enough compromise for the two of them. Panda's thoughts occasionally wandered back to their bag, praying it was safe from prying eyes.

Within thirty minutes, they were at the mall, but when they went inside, everything looked washed out. Drew noticed that the majority of the stores were closed, probably unable to compete with online shopping. The layout was simple enough to follow in a U-shape. Drew was convinced the revenue from the food court and the punk and anime shops were enough to keep the lights on. Window shopping and grazing around the food court somehow kept teens like them occupied for hours.

"Have you guys gotten your tuxes yet?" Wynter bounced over to a boutique shop that displayed elegant dresses for prom season. The bright lights from within made Drew's eyes slant.

"Got mine last weekend," Trey beamed triumphantly.

"Uh huh," Wynter crossed her arms. "And what color scheme has the princess commanded?"

"Purple." He rolled his eyes.

"And you're all set?"

Trey sucked on his teeth. "She's getting my tie and stuff. She's worried I'll get the wrong SHADE." His face twisted as he recited his girlfriend's vocabulary.

The pair snickered under their breath. "Hell has frozen over," Wynter declared. "I'm agreeing with the Devil's spawn. You would get the wrong shade. Drew? Have you got your tux?"

"I just agreed to go to prom an hour ago," Panda grumbled. "What do you think?" Drew sighed.

And with that, Drew and Trey found themselves neck deep in satin. Wynter was so excited that she didn't hear Drew say he'd rent one instead of buying a six-hundred-dollar suit for one night. He had to repeat it three times before she heard him.

She dragged the guys across the hall to the men's formal wear department anyway. Drew's discomfort was at an all-time high as a thin, older woman worked to find his size. Her professional fingers caused his skin distress beneath his clothes as she tightened the fabric against him, gauging his options.

Soon, he went into the dressing room with a third pair of pants over his arm. His self-esteem quickly depleted as he stared at his reflection, not to mention how horrid his scars looked under the fluorescent lights in the changing room, or how his skin chafed against the foreign material. These pants were also too long by an inch. And his overcoat was extra-large. He looked like a boy who'd gotten into his dad's wardrobe. *"What if we borrowed one of Dad's suits anyways? We're bound to fit his size better than this."* Drew shot daggers at Panda. *"Right, sorry. Touched too close to creepy, even for me."*

Drew emerged and looked at Wynter, who shook her head in thought. "This is what happens when you leave things to the last second." She held her chin between her thumb and the knuckle of her forefinger and her lips pushed to the side as she racked her brain for a solution. Then she turned and spoke to the snippy employee on Drew's behalf.

Drew looked at himself in the mirror. His humiliated eyes wandered over to the reflection of Trey, whose wide chest appeared pinched when he crossed his bulking arms. When Trey finally caught Drew's eyes in the mirror, Drew threw on a dramatic face, straining his neck and widening his eyes. "HELP ME!" he mouthed. Trey laughed at his friend's distress. *"Why can't we just show up in a clean pair of jeans?"* Panda lamented.

Wynter turned from the employee. The annoyed crease between her brows vanished when she looked at him. "So, I can pin your pants easily. My dad's got a jacket you can borrow if you want. And as for the button up…"

"I've got one," Drew answered a little too quickly. Panda winced at the suggestion. *"I hope it still fits if we're thinking of the same green button up from Dad's winter gala three years ago. And if it does fit, I don't want to wear it!"*

Wynter slapped on a tight-lipped smile and returned to the unfortunate employee stuck helping three teenagers who really didn't know what they were doing. Drew hurriedly returned to the changing room. He kicked off the clothes as if they were burning him alive. The material felt restrictive and the overcoat threatened to swallow him whole.

"We can't borrow Wynter's dad's clothes!! That's worse than using Dad's!" Panda wailed.

Drew stopped. His chin touched his chest as he looked down. The pants pooled at his feet. It looked like a black hole. If only it'd swallow him whole. Maybe he could borrow his dad's stuff. "I mean…WE could? Mom hasn't cleared out his closet yet," Drew shrugged at Panda. "Maybe it'd be like, honoring our dad or something. It'd be better than dealing with all of this." Drew looked around the changing room. The walls were starting to cave in and the room was shrinking by the second.

Panda shook his head in disbelief. "*Whatever you gotta tell yourself, dude.*" Drew bent down to retrieve his phone from the back pocket of his jeans. His fingers hovered over the screen, thinking about what to say. How to say it? He decided to finish getting dressed before he sent it.

DREW: Prom is next weekend. Would it be alright if I borrowed something from Dad?

CELESTE: Of course! How exciting. We can go through it tonight if you want.

DREW: Do you think his clothes would fit?

CELESTE: Absolutely. And if not, maybe you could raid your uncle's closet?

Drew's body went rigid reading his mom's last text. He didn't bother responding to it. Now that he was fully dressed, he felt better. His distressed scars were quiet again. He sloppily returned the formal clothes to their hangers. On his way out of the dressing room, he handed them to the woman with an apologetic smile, "Sorry, I'm good."

Panda started to hyperventilate and humiliation clawed at

Drew's neck. They had to get out of that store. Drew scurried out, not caring if his friends followed. They did, of course. After letting Drew wander around a bit, the three finally found solace in the food court. Panda's breathing returned to normal while Trey and Wynter made idle chatter. To Drew's relief, they left him out of it. The area was fairly quiet for a Sunday afternoon. Drew picked at his fries. Panda hogged his chicken nuggets. Trey pulled on his smoothie straw, and Wynter, across the table, timidly bit into her burger.

"So..." she chipmunked her food for a moment. One cheek puffed out as she spoke. "You're going with Ms. Perfect," she pointed at Trey. Looking at Drew, she asked, "Would you want to go together?" Drew and Panda completely missed the slight blush to Wynter's cheeks.

"Don't you mean Devil's spawn?" Trey remarked from her snide comment earlier.

Wynter stuck her tongue out at him and scrunched up her nose. She gently tapped Drew in the leg with her foot. The gentle nudge had the full force of a soccer kick, shocking Drew back into focus. Seeing the disordered look on his face, she repeated her question. "Did you want to go together?" Her confidence faltered for a minute.

"Where?" Drew's brow creased. Panda slapped his forehead over Drew's obliviousness.

Wynter blinked at him with growing impatience. "To prom?"

"Oh, I was thinking maybe…" Drew's eyes fell to his fries. "I want to ask Miranda!" Panda announced before Drew could stop him.

"Dude!" Trey slapped him on the back like a proud parent. "Wait, you mean you haven't asked her yet?"

Wynter's face fell in betrayal. "For real?" her voice echoed in pain.

Drew's shy smile dropped at her reaction. Panda rubbed at his temples. His words channeled out of Drew's mouth, "You know what? I don't get your problem with Miranda. Sydney, I get." He held a hand up at Trey, "No offense, dude." Trey just rolled his eyes at the ancient argument. Drew continued, "Sydney isn't very nice, but you don't even know Miranda."

"I know her better than you do," Wynter's jaw clenched.

Drew threw his fry on the table. "What horrible thing did she do to you?"

Wynter opened her mouth to speak. Her lips twitched. Then she changed her mind and closed her mouth.

"No really," Panda continued to goad, "I'm dying to know why you hate her and Porter so damn much!"

"Because they started those rumors that I'm a slut!" Wynter blurted out. Her grey eyes looked like a violent storm.

Drew's and Trey's shoulders slouched and Wynter's nose flared widely as she tried to resist her angry tears.

"What?" Drew exhaled in shocked disbelief.

Wynter sighed in exhaustion. "Remember when I was Coach Hoyt's TA last year?" Everyone silently nodded.

"Didn't you quit, like, a week into it?" Trey leaned forward, resting his enormous arms on the table.

Wynter's brows raised in a no shit-gesture. "At the end of seventh, he needed the locker rooms checked to make sure personal items weren't left behind and any equipment was returned to the storage room. It's a quick check that takes less than five minutes." She mumbled the last part to herself. Drew leaned forward, reducing the space between the three of them. Wynter shook her head and continued, "I thought I was alone in the boy's locker. But Ricky had gotten there early for practice."

"Ricky Vitale?" Trey interrupted. Rage scrunched his face up.

Wynter nodded. "He hit on me. I initially ignored him, but he backed me into a corner." She shook her head, dismissing the memories, but she could still feel how his hands weighed like bricks on her hips and his handcuff grip on her wrists when he pinned them to her side after she had tried to shove him off of her. She continued, "Porter, Goodman, and some other guy came in. Their interruption gave me my getaway. But not without hearing Porter's bitchy comment to me. And your Ms. Goody-Two-Shoes did nothing!" She looked at Drew and sat back, crossing her arms. Drew could feel how angry and upset she was.

"Wyn…"

"What did Sydney say?" Trey interrupted.

"It doesn't matter. I've told you guys all year how awful those girls are! Now do you believe me?" She shook her head, scoffing. "Just take me home, Trey." She stood up, not giving them a choice.

Drew trailed behind Trey and Wynter. He could see Wynter's anger rolling off her in waves, her arms crossed tightly across her chest as she led them to the car. He nearly ran into Trey as his hulking friend stopped right in front of him. "Maybe it should just be me to drop her off?" Trey said quietly.

"What am I supposed to do?" Drew threw his arms out in defense.

Trey shrugged, his face twisted with discomfort. Drew hated when they fought like this. It didn't happen often, but when it did, it felt like the end of the world. "She's really pissed, man," Trey's back straightened as he heard his car door slam behind him. "I'll be right back for you. Her house is practically down the street."

Before Drew could argue any further, Trey turned and jogged to his car, got in, and quickly peeled out of the parking lot. Drew found a seat on the bench by the entrance. Panda sat beside him.

"We don't really believe Wynter, do we?"

"How can we not?" Drew rubbed his hand over his face.

"I don't doubt Porter was a total bitch to Wynter when all that happened." Panda propped his elbows up on the back of the bench. *"But we know Miranda. She wouldn't do something like that."*

Drew replayed every conversation, every interaction he had with Miranda as Panda continued, *"She's kind. Nicer to us than half our school. She's great with Evie. Miranda makes us feel safe. She's easy to talk to."*

"So is Wynter," Drew sighed.

"Wynter is not easy to talk to. I feel like all she does is nag us."

Drew shook his head in disagreement. "That's because she knows us. She wants what's best for us. I don't blame her for being sick of our shit."

"Miranda knows us."

Drew squinted over at the furry creature beside him. "Does she really?"

"It's not like you've divulged every ugly secret to Wynter either." Panda cocked his head at him. *"Girls are just mean to each other. It's what they do. I don't think that should change what we've got going on with Miranda."*

Drew quietly waited for Trey to come back to get him. The internal war with himself continued as he tried to defend Wynter and Panda took up Miranda's side. Trey soon pulled up, and Drew got in the passenger seat with the enthusiasm of a zombie.

"Jesus dude," Trey huffed out as they made their way back to Drew's house.

"That bad?" Drew winced.

"It was painfully quiet. I thought she'd bite my head off if I said something. Do you think the girls would really do that? That Vitale actually came on to her like that?"

Drew shrugged in guilt. "She's our friend, right?

Shouldn't we take her side?" His head rolled over to look at Trey. The awful rumors swam around his head. "*Everyone called her 'Quick Winter',*" Panda reminded him. Drew thought the stupid gossip had died down. "*It doesn't absolve the residual trauma left behind. You, of all people, should know better!*" Panda chastised. Drew rubbed at his face and groaned. "You going to talk to Sydney?"

"Damn straight I am." Trey's brows were stern with anger. "I know Sydney doesn't get along with some people. But I never thought she'd be a bully. What about Miranda? Are you going to talk to her?"

Drew could feel Panda's intense stare, willing him to defend Miranda. "*Go ahead, she's not one of your best friends you've known for almost five years.*" Drew let out a deep breath. "I don't know. According to Wynter, Miranda didn't say anything."

"Isn't lack of action just as bad?" Trey looked over at him in confusion. Drew only had the energy to shrug again.

CHAPTER TWELVE

That night was slow for Drew. *"We've oversaturated the market,"* Panda criticized. It was Panda's idea to continue selling off the rest of their supply in Wallace's territory, so the two were downtown again. Last weekend was a success. But tonight, on a Sunday, it was slow. Panda occupied their time by replaying everything that had happened at the mall earlier that afternoon on repeat.

"Would you shut up?" Drew groaned. "Take a break. Or at least think of something else."

"I can't!" Panda remembered the look on Wynter's face. Drew felt sick to his stomach. What was it Panda had called it? *"Friendship treason!"* Panda reminded him.

"Right," Drew scoffed, rolling his eyes.

"What do we do about Miranda?" Panda contemplated.

"There's nothing to do." Drew glanced at him, "I'm still going to ask her to prom. That's it."

"*That's not it though, is it?*" Panda pushed. "*Going to prom wasn't the plan. The plan was to stick to the Econ class project.*"

Drew swallowed, his throat dry. "But we like her."

Panda shrugged, kicking a rock away. "*We like Wynter too.*" Drew ignored that admission. He was growing troubled with his uncertainty in not knowing exactly who to pick. He wasn't in the mood to play Panda's game. "*Do you really think Miranda is just as bad as Porter?*" Drew didn't answer. He'd been asking himself the same thing all night.

The sudden buzzing in his pocket caused Drew's heart to jump. He pulled his phone out and immediately answered. It was Trey.

"*Is he ok?*" Panda asked as Drew greeted his friend. "*He never calls.*"

"Hey dude," Trey sounded tired. His voice seemed thick over the line. "You at home?"

"Um..." Drew looked around and focused on the curb corner where he was standing. It had taken him almost an hour to get here on his bike. "I'm downtown."

"Can I come out?"

Drew stiffened. Trey always kept Drew at arm's length

when he was selling. Drew couldn't blame him for wanting to stay away from the dealing side of the business. Trey had only ever been involved by encouraging Drew to bring some weed over for his parties. It was a win-win for them both—customers for Drew and increased popularity for Trey. Apprehensively, Drew finally told Trey which intersection he was at. "*Something's wrong.*" Panda began pacing in concern.

It took Trey only twenty minutes to get there by car. The two struggled to shove Drew's bike in the trunk. "Do you mind if I hang here with you for a while before we head home?" Trey asked.

"*Ask him what's wrong.*" Panda bugged repeatedly. But Drew kept his mouth in a tight line as he nodded. Trey watched silently as Drew sold a baggie of uppers here and there. The pair silently walked up and down the main street, Drew with his backpack visible to all and Trey with his hands in his pockets, quiet. Drew agreed with Panda, something was definitely wrong with his friend. Trey's broad shoulders were slumped in defeat. His eyes were red and puffy. "*Has he been crying?*"

"How long are you going to keep doing this?" Trey eventually asked after a customer walked away.

The question caught Drew by surprise. He'd argued the point with Wynter countless times. Trey, though, had an out of sight, out of mind mentality when it came to Drew.

Drew shrugged, "I'm working on getting out actually."

"Really?"

Drew nodded, "This is what I have left for Omar." He held his bag open so his friend could peer inside. There was less than a handful of weed and uppers left. Drew was hoping to sell off what little he had left during prom night.

Trey shook his head, resuming his stoic stance. Drew tensed at his friend's dismissal. Panda bristled as well, feeling defensive of his decision to push Drew to be in rival gang's territory on a Sunday night. They should be at home, playing video games, keeping an eye on Evie, and studying for finals. Drew knew he should be anywhere instead of where he was right now, doing what he was doing. Even Panda couldn't argue with that.

"I actually talked to Omar yesterday."

"Oh?" Trey raised a surprised brow.

"He said if I sold off the rest of this shit then I'm out."

Trey looked at him doubtfully. "Why didn't you say something sooner? Wynter would've been so stoked to hear that. You know how she feels about it."

Drew looked off to the side. "I wanted to focus on her. She'd just told us about the program. I didn't want to take that away from her and make it all about me."

Trey nodded in understanding and then resumed his subdued stance.

"Why are you here, man?" Drew sighed. "*Yeah! Why IS he here?*" Panda worryingly echoed. "What's going on?" Drew finally asked, trying to quiet Panda's annoyance before he blurted out something inappropriate.

Trey sighed heavily. He couldn't make eye contact. His breath shuddered. "I, uh, Sydney and I broke up." His voice broke on her name.

Drew's eyes widened at this news. "What! Why? What happened?" Panda's questions fired out of Drew. Panda's defenses fell and he felt bad for Trey. Drew decided to quietly hang back and wait patiently for the story to unfold.

It felt like minutes passed as they all walked in silence before Trey finally answered. "I thought a lot about what Wynter told us today. I had to know for certain what happened. After I dropped you off, I asked Sydney to come over so I could talk to her."

"Yeah?"

"I sat her down and asked her if she remembered that day

in the locker room." Drew kept his mouth closed, even though he was burning to know what happened. "She said she saw Wynter all over Vitale." Trey took a deep breath. "Sydney said that Wynter had always been a bitch to her and that she was just telling everyone what she saw, that is…'Wynter being a slut.'" Trey shivered as he recited Sydney's words.

"She said that about Wynter?" Drew asked in disbelief.

"I know Wynter and Sydney never got along. That's some beef that goes back to middle school." Trey shook his head. "I just couldn't believe Sydney would gossip like that. Even seeing it from her point of view, IF she saw Wynter as the one who was coming on to Vitale. Even if that's true, Sydney should never have helped spread the gossip."

"And then what happened?"

Trey blinked as if he were getting over the sadness part of his breakup and moving on to the next steps of grief and anger. "I told her as much. That spreading those rumors about Wynter and name calling was really hurtful. You remember how Wynter was?"

Drew nodded, vividly remembering how Wynter used to come over to his house in tears about how cruel everyone was. Her online accounts had blown up with girls calling her ugly names and boys treating her like a prostitute for hire. It took months for the bullying to lose steam, but the occasional snide comments never stopped.

"Then Sydney started yelling at me. She said that I was taking sides with the 'goth freak' over her. That Wynter had it coming…" Trey shut his mouth as a stranger walked by. When they were alone again, he resumed, "I couldn't believe how mean Sydney was being. I told her that Wynter was my friend. That no one deserves to be bullied like she had been. I told her that I wanted her to try and be nicer to Wynter. Water under the bridge, ya know?"

Drew nodded his head in understanding as a customer approached. Trey stepped back, his hands in his pockets, and waited in silence until the stranger was taken care of and on their way. He stood next to Drew again and continued, "Sydney said I had to pick…either her or Wynter."

"And you picked Wynter," Drew answered gently.

Trey groaned. His brow furrowed in thought and his jaw clenched. "I didn't answer her right away. That made Sydney even angrier. I couldn't handle the ultimatum. I didn't want to pick between either of them. I just wanted them to be nicer to each other. I get that they hate each other and that obviously they wouldn't be doing each other's hair or painting their nails or whatever it is that girls do. But I really wanted them to get along for my sake. So, instead of answering Sydney, I said, 'What now?'" Trey took another deep breath and his fists clenched.

"She said she needed a man who would support her one thousand percent. She seemed so angry at me. I was just in shock that she even said that to me! I just couldn't pick between Sydney and Wynter. I still can't!" Trey rubbed his face in frustration. "She said I wasn't man enough for her, and then she left." He exhaled sharply.

Drew patted his friend on the back, bringing him in close by the shoulders. Behind them, Panda began calling Sydney every offensive thing he could think of, mouthing the words so as not to distract Drew, who was already angry at how deeply she hurt his best friend. Trey took in another breath, this one a bit steadier. Drew wanted to say how much Sydney was a bully from the beginning and how he had never liked her. But none of that would make his friend feel better.

Instead, Drew decided to say, "You're a good man. It's her own fault for not seeing that."

Trey sniffed hard and nodded at Drew. The pair straightened up and continued their walk. Trey stared off into the distance as if he were reliving every interaction he had with Sydney over the course of their relationship. They had gotten together at the end of Freshman year. *"Holy crap,"* Panda did the math. *"That's gotta be two years they were together."* Drew agreed that was forever in high school math.

Drew saw off another customer. When they were alone again, he asked Trey, "Did you ever love her?"

Trey sighed loudly, "I think I did. I never actually said it out loud though."

Drew thought about Trey's past relationships. The first girlfriend he had was in the seventh grade and it lasted two weeks. The one after that lasted a month and so on. Trey had a revolving door of girls. But they never seemed serious. In the beginning, Drew didn't take him and Sydney seriously either. He thought she was more of a hook up for Trey than anything. Then six months passed, Trey's longest record at the time, and Porter was still around. It was like she had completely consumed Trey, keeping him away from Drew and Wynter.

Last year Trey made more of an effort to hang out with them. Drew appreciated his efforts. He'd missed his best friend. And he was thankful that Trey was there to support him when his dad passed away and during his house arrest. It seemed like hanging out with Trey had gotten a little easier after he got his car and was able to drive himself places when Porter didn't demand his attention.

"How can you be with someone for two years and not love them?" Panda asked in confusion.

"Why do you think you were with her for so long?"

Trey stared up at the black sky. "She wasn't bad in middle school."

Drew didn't necessarily agree with that. Porter had always been obsessed with being the center of attention. He thought when they got to high school, she had just become more aggressive with being in the spotlight.

"She's pretty. She was nice to me and supportive," Trey continued. "I know she's on the cheerleading squad. So, they have to come to our games. But I swear I could hear her cheering louder for me. She made me feel good about my-self. And I guess, I was never alone when I was with her."

"That's because she was so clingy with you," Panda grumbled out before Drew could stop him.

"I know. And looking back on it, I'm not sure if that was really healthy." Trey shrugged, "I don't know, man. I think I was so present with her that I didn't plan out a future with her. She made me feel good when I was with her. And that was enough for me."

Trey's words replayed over and over in Drew's head. He could completely understand what Trey was saying. It reminded him of how he felt about Miranda. Drew did like her. He liked spending time with her. But could he really open himself up to her and share the deepest, darkest parts of himself with her? Could he ever tell her about the place where Panda was born from?

Drew suddenly snapped out of his thoughts when a man stepped up to him. Trey backed away to give them some space. "Yo, you sellin'?" Drew felt the man's hot breath on his face. He resisted scrunching up his face as the stranger's stale breath hit him in the nose.

"Does this guy look familiar to you?" Panda wondered, squinting at the new customer. Drew nodded and looked at his backpack. "Yeah, whatcha' need? I've got weed and uppers."

The man jerked his chin up. "Let me get a quarter of weed."

Drew nodded and then fished in his backpack for the bag. When he pulled it out, the man seized his wrist. The calloused hand chafed Drew's slim wrist and he panicked, his eyes bugging out. He felt Trey behind him, ready to tackle them both if need be.

"Who do you think you are, sellin' on our turf?" the man accused.

"Oh shit!" Drew gasped. "*It's one of Wallace's thugs!*" Panda wailed.

"Aye, yo! I've got one!" the man called out loudly.

"*Shit!*" Panda and Drew knew that if they didn't get out of there fast, they'd be overrun by Wallace's gang. Drew tried to yank his wrist free, but the thug just tightened his grip. Suddenly, Trey was there. Like a bullet, his fist flew through the air, landing squarely on the man's jaw. Drew pulled away the moment the grip loosened.

"Run!" Drew yelled at a terrified Trey. Without another word, they all sprinted toward the direction of Trey's car.

"What the hell, man?!" Trey yelled from behind him.

Drew couldn't answer him just yet. He turned, leading them down an alley, hoping it was a short cut to Trey's car. Looking back, he could see at least three of Wallace's men running after them.

Drew inhaled sharply. "Get your keys ready!"

Trey fumbled with his hand in his pocket, careful not to drop his keys. The sound of sneakers hitting the sidewalk echoed against the alley walls. Drew could hear their pursuers grunting behind them as they attempted to catch up.

"Hey!" one of them called. "No one sells on Wallace's turf and gets away with it!"

This only made Drew and Trey run faster, harder. Drew's arms swung wildly as he pushed himself. His ribs started to cramp. His heart thundered in his ears. *"We've got to get rid of these guys!"* Panda yelled from Drew's side. They sprinted across the intersection just as their light turned red. Trey gasped as oncoming cars accelerated toward him from both directions, but he easily dodged each one. A few of the cars honked at them once they got to the other side of the street. The thick traffic created the distance they needed. Drew cut through another alley just to throw the thugs off. After darting through one more intersection, they could see Trey's car. The flashing headlights, signaling it was un-locked, were a beacon of salvation as they ran up on it.

Drew and Trey jumped in and slammed their doors. Drew swiveled his head around, keeping a lookout for the guys while Trey started the car and quickly pulled out. Heavy panting filled the car. Drew saw them stumbling out of an alley as Trey drove away. Drew quickly gave directions how to get out of downtown, out of Wallace's territory. They took the long way home, crisscrossing three extra streets in case someone was following them. Drew didn't want an ambush from Wallace's men. "We're good, dude," Drew exhaled. "Just take this street back up until you hit Pine Street and then…"

"Who the hell was that?!" Trey interrupted, half yelling. Drew looked down at Trey's hands on the steering wheel. Trey was gripping it so hard that his knuckles had turned white. "Is that what you go through?"

Drew quickly shook his head, "Not usually…"

"Then why were those guys chasing us?"

"Because we were in another guy's territory." Drew stretched his head to the side, hearing some of the bones in his neck crack.

"Why were we in another guy's territory?" Trey yelled again. "I punched that guy! Am I in danger? Will they come after me now?"

Drew pinched the bridge of his nose, trying to think of some way to calm his friend down. "You're safe. They don't know who we are." Drew took a deep breath, "Thanks for having my back…"

"This is why I don't get involved with your shit!" Trey interrupted.

"Whoa!" Panda snapped his head to the driver. "I'm not the one who asked you to come out."

"It's freaking dangerous, Drew. I don't understand why you do it."

"I'm trying to get out," Panda attempted to explain.

"By selling more shit? That's your idea of getting out?" Trey interrupted again.

Panda was red in the face. Drew was unable to stop Panda's rant, "You don't get it! Omar took me in after my dad died!"

"I was there!" Trey shot back, speeding a little too fast down the road. "So was Wynter! You had US!"

Drew inhaled sharply. He released his breath before Panda could retort. Trey was right. Drew did have his friends after his dad passed. But Drew was so sick of the condolences and the grief at the time.

An old classmate who graduated had introduced Drew to Omar. Drew liked that Omar didn't treat him with kid gloves. He wasn't worried if Drew was going to break down crying. Omar kept Drew busy. So busy that Drew didn't have time to mourn his dad. And then the money he earned started to roll in. He didn't want out back then.

Now he did. He didn't want to stress his mom and friends out any more than they already were. He wanted to honor his dad's memory. He wanted to prove his uncle wrong and show him that he wasn't a drug-dealing failure. He didn't want to get busted again and go to jail. He wanted to be better for Evie. Drew wanted to be better for himself. Drew sighed, losing the last bits of his anger. "You're right."

Trey's grip on the wheel softened.

"Trust me, I've got a plan. I'm over all of it too, man." Drew heaved a heavy sigh.

Trey sighed too, releasing the last bits of his tension.

CHAPTER THIRTEEN

Drew's heart thumped hard. "*What do we do with our hands? Why did we let her do this?*" Panda's anxiety only added to his own. A sea of indifferent eyes stared at the two of them. Drew noted that Mrs. Mallard had given up her normal chair behind the massive teacher desk in order to sit at the very back of the Econ class where she could take in every project as a whole. Panda noted that she took constructive notes after every slide.

Both Panda and Drew were aware that they had Mrs. Mallard's undivided attention. And Trey's attention, to Drew's temporary relief. Panda worked hard to ignore Sydney's glare. Her arms were crossed and a scowl lined her face. Drew worried for a moment how Trey's project would go now that he and Sydney had broken up. "*Let's focus on our presentation first,"* Panda reminded, getting Drew back on track.

The typically chilled room was boiling. Drew felt like his nerves were going to choke him when Miranda started their presentation. He looked at the presentation slides for the first time as she spoke in a clear, auditory voice. He assumed it was her cheerleader personality that was driving her today. Panda's unease turned mean. *"I hate public speaking. Everyone is watching us! Don't mess up."*

Drew's heart paused for a moment in dread when Miranda stopped talking. *"Shit, it's our turn!"* Drew cleared Panda out of the way for his own voice and began.

"Based off our combined budget…we plan on investing in three different areas…A mutual fund with an upfront cost of $10,000. This is a one-time expense that will continue to accrue interest without any additional action from us. We can, of course, choose to add more money if we want, but assuming we only do this as a once off thing…if we do this when we turn 18, by the time we turn 65, we'll have earned $470,000."

Drew took a shaky breath as he continued. Miranda clicked onto the next slides for him. "Our next step would be to invest in real estate…Our population has continued to steadily increase for the last fifty years. Real estate continues to be a valuable commodity in this area. There are first-time home buyer programs that we can use separately on two different homes. One for us to live in and one to rent. Rent earned will go toward the mortgage until it's fully paid off and to other home repairs. At that time, we can choose either to sell it for a lump sum amount or keep it for a steady monthly income, continuing to rent it out."

"Almost done! Keep going!" Panda cheered. Drew managed to keep his eyes roaming throughout the room during his presentation, mainly bouncing back and forth between Trey and Mrs. Mallard. Trey gave him a thumbs up. With that encouragement, Drew took an even breath.

"And lastly, will be tangible goods. For me personally, I understand the value of collectable items. By buying high-end, vintage comics, I intend to preserve them and resell them. Take for example this comic book. When first released in 1973, it was worth 20 cents. When I bought it two years ago it was worth $1,500. Following this rate of value, by the time I am 65 years old, it will be worth $9.4 million. Miranda has told me that she plans on using her own paintings to turn a profit. Not as big an exponential growth as the comic book, but still disposable income while doing something she loves."

As Drew came to his last slide, his back was straighter. He'd found his stride during the presentation. "These are smaller investments than mutual funds and real estate. But it is a hobby of ours. Collecting, tracking value, and painting. These hobbies will be used to pay for fun things like vacations. Gravy money that we're able to turn around and use as a reward."

Miranda smiled when it was her turn to finish with their conclusion. "Life should be used to experience it. And to experience it, we also have to be prepared. By starting our investment plan early with the money we have right now, we will be in a better financial position than our predecessors. All while having the financial means to enjoy the little things in life. Something as small as going to the movies, to more grandiose adventures like amusement parks, and world travel."

END OF SLIDE PRESENTATION

The students clapped flatly upon seeing the black slide. Mrs. Mallard nodded, impressed at the pair. Miranda smiled encouragingly at Drew. One corner of his mouth tugged up, thankful it was over. Panda proudly patted him on the back. Drew was just grateful they didn't embarrass themselves.

"Thank you Drew and Miranda," Mrs. Mallard gripped her clip board. "Can you tell me who did what?"

"I did slides one through five and ten and Drew did six through nine."

"Whose idea was it for the investment plan?"

Miranda wrung her fingers a bit before answering. "Well, I thought of a government bond or CDs, but Drew thought the mutual fund would be better. My mom is a real estate agent, so I understand that market. And it was Drew's idea to profit off our hobbies."

"And you did a combined budget? Why?" Something in Mrs. Mallard's question made Drew's stomach twist. It didn't come out mean. But her curiosity could've easily been mistaken for judgement.

Miranda looked to Drew for an answer. He was perfectly happy to let her talk the whole time. *"But we're feeling brave today."* Panda shrugged, "Do you make the majority of your financial decisions, Mrs. Mallard? Or do you consult your husband? Pool your money together? Our plan can work separately or together. But we figured most households work with a combined income." A few of his classmates "oohed" hearing Drew stand up to their teacher.

She cleared her throat, quieting the room. Her lips

turned down in surprised amusement. "Fair enough," she said as she jotted some notes. "Alright, thanks guys. Raquel, Stephanie, and Mikayla. You're up."

Drew returned to his desk as Miranda clicked out of the shared drive for the next group. Trey gave him a high five with a happy smile. Panda released his tense breath. Miranda sat down beside him, releasing a heavy breath. If she was nervous during the presentation, she didn't show it. She reached over and rested a hand on his arm. Panda went rigid at her surprise touch, willing her hand to stay there forever. The warmth of her palm traveled along his entire nervous system, heating his whole body. Her vibrant, chestnut eyes shined brightly. She turned and said a silent "thank you." Normally, Miranda was taken advantage of during projects and had to do all the work. Drew felt ashamed that he didn't practice or do any of the final touch ups for the PowerPoint, but Miranda was just thankful she didn't do ALL of it.

She leaned back in her chair and quietly retrieved a book from her bag. Drew smiled because he half expected her to spend this time studying. In fact, he should be using this time to study for his next final, too. Panda patted him on the back in encouragement. *"How brave are we really feeling today?"*

Drew quietly reached into his backpack for his phone. He

scrolled to find his text chat with Miranda, and then shot her a message. He stared in astonishment as she pulled her phone out of a discreet pocket in her dress. *"That thing has pockets?!"* Panda noted with excitement. She smiled down at her phone. Drew could feel himself sweating. His heart was being put through its paces today. He tried to read her reaction out of the corner of his eye.

He glanced down at his phone. Anticipation ate away at his insides. Three dots popped up twice before disappearing. *"But what about Wynter?"* Panda made Drew second guess what he had texted. With a creased forehead, Drew gripped his phone tighter. He glanced sideways at Miranda and his face turned hard as he took in her dress. Mint green. It was a beautiful shade paired with her dark, wavy hair. But his stomach twisted at the color. He loved Miranda in dresses. But this was by far his least favorite.

He snapped out of it when her wide eyes flicked to him. Drew eyes were glued. He didn't look away. Then his phone buzzed in his hand. He snapped his head down to read the incoming text.

DREW: Will you go to prom with me?

MIRANDA: Yes

Panda exhaled a little too loudly. But Drew didn't care.

Miranda's lips curled inward and she moved the book up to her face, hiding her blush. Drew didn't think a three-letter word could bring him so much delight. For the first time since he had dropped Evie off at school that morning, he smiled. Unable to contain his happiness, he turned his head to a rosy Miranda.

"I just hope our colors aren't green!" Panda shouted with glee.

CHAPTER FOURTEEN

The one positive to Finals Week were the half days. Tomorrow was Friday, the day for seventh period's finals. It was also a makeup day. Since Drew didn't have a seventh period and had finished all his other finals, he was basically done with his Junior year. Prom was also on Friday and Monday was his official last day of school. He would get his report card at the end-of-year assembly where the whole school sent the seniors off with academic and athletic awards and celebrated each grade as they moved up. Then, it was locker clean-out and yearbook signing. Yeah, he was basically done. Graduation for the seniors was Tuesday. He didn't really know any seniors, so he didn't see a point in going to the graduation ceremony.

Because it was a half day, Drew was enjoying having the

house to himself, thankful that Liam and his mom were busy at work. Drew still had two hours before he had to go get Evie. With a bowl of chips in front of him and the TV on just to fill the house with noise, Drew lazily scrolled through his phone as he lounged, sprawled out on the couch. Something on the TV briefly caught his attention before his eyes were drawn back down to his phone. But Drew had the sinking feeling he wasn't alone. His dad's ghost kept staring at him from the corner of the room on the curio shelf. Photos, medals, and a neatly folded flag screamed at Drew. He tried to shrug off the cold shiver he was getting. A nagging feeling ate at his insides, not allowing him to enjoy this rare moment of solitude. It was Panda. He'd been quiet since Drew got home.

Drew groaned. "What's the problem?"

"*With what?*" Panda kept his eyes on his phone. He sat on the floor with his legs crossed, leaning against the couch.

"Why are you brooding?" He sat up.

Panda snorted. "*I'm not doing anything. What's your problem?*"

"Nothing! I had a great day today."

"*Sure...*"

"I know I passed my finals..."

Panda twisted his face condescendingly, "*Could've studied more.*"

"Miranda said yes to prom!"

Panda shrugged. "*Since when do you care about prom?*"

"I don't," Drew jeered, "but this is the first step toward something more."

"*How can she be more when you're a screw-up? You don't even know what you want. Especially when you hate your own mind, your own skin.*" Panda looked at him. His eyes were cold with spite.

Drew snapped. "Because of you! You don't know what YOU want! You're the one who keeps changing his mind. You're the one who pushed me to be with Miranda. You're the one who cut me up in the first place!"

Panda scoffed. "*You really are dumb. I'm only here because of you. You're the one in control, Drew! Yet I get blamed for every-thing.*"

Drew flinched at his words. "Because it's your fault! I hate you!"

"*And yet, you need me,*" Panda gleamed at him.

"I don't need you."

"*More than you think. Why do you think I'm here? I protect you. I support you.*"

Drew shook his head in doubt. "When do you ever support me?"

A large photo of his dad in uniform watched him. His dad's smile seemed forced. His eyes tight. The criticism transcended from beyond the grave, whirling around Drew's head in mockery:

How could I have such an UGLY son? A DUMB one at that, too. I can't believe I DIED to protect you. How can you PROTECT your sister when you can't even protect yourself? Letting your mother work herself to DEATH? A stupid, good for nothing drug dealer. You are NOTHING. WORTHLESS!

Drew leaned forward and covered his ears. He rocked gently, attempting to soothe himself and quiet the vile words. Panda sat on the floor, gently stroking at Drew's knee. Panda's words laced between his father's. *"We're doing our best,"* Panda calmed. *"We are loved. We have friends. Our family needs us."*

"Would you stop?!" Drew stood up, kicking Panda away.

"I'm just trying to make you feel better!" Panda shouted back as he stood up.

"By making me feel like shit first?"

"Maybe…" Panda swayed his body side to side, clasping

his hands together, "...*you should take some fucking res-*
ponsibility!" Drew scoffed and turned away from him. "*Reality*
check, Drew!" Panda continued, waving his arms wildly in the
air. "*This is all in your head!*"

Fuming, Drew grabbed the bowl of chips, turned off the
TV, and started making his way toward the basement stairs.
He was trying to distance himself from the noise raging in his
mind.

"*You can't keep putting your shit on me, dude!*" Panda continued to yell behind him.

The sound of the garage door opening on the other side
of the wall made Drew jump. His shoulders slouched in
relief. Celeste's weary eyes pulsed with life when she walked
in the door and saw him.

"Hey," she sighed. "What are you up to?"

"Just heading downstairs." He shook the bowl of chips in
his arms, causing a soft rustle to echo into the room.

Her head cocked to the side. "No school?"

"It's Finals Week."

"Oh," she still seemed confused about what Finals Week
had to do with him being home early.

"What about you?" Drew interrupted.

"I've got the afternoon off. Figured I could get a nap

before getting Evie."

"I'll be downstairs then." He turned and got halfway down the stairwell before he heard his mom rush to the top of the stairs.

"Hey! Isn't prom tomorrow? Did you go through your dad's closet?"

Panda cringed. "*Oh, BAD timing.*"

Drew tried to swallow the lump in his throat, but it didn't budge. He half turned to his mom. Avoiding her eyes, he said, "Not yet."

"You're running out of time," she half chuckled. "Why don't we look right now?"

"But your nap…"

"I'll sleep when I'm dead," she gave him a small smile.

"That's not funny," Drew answered flatly.

Her small smile dropped immediately. "No," she cleared her throat, "you're right. Sorry." Her brows knitted in the middle. "You know what I mean."

Drew set the bowl of chips down on a stair and pinched the bridge of his nose, trying to calm himself from his fight with Panda. "Mom, I really don't feel like it right now."

She dropped her hands against her thighs. "There will never be a good time, Drew. And if we don't find anything, then you and I can run to the store and see if they have anything available."

Drew's stomach dropped at the thought of clothes shopping with his mom. It was cringe worthy enough with his two best friends there. It'd surely be worse with his mom present.

He groaned, "Ugh, Mom…"

"Come on," Celeste took a step back from the edge of the stairs. "Best to just rip it off like a Band-Aid. We'll be quick with it."

Drew stared at Celeste for a few beats, trying to will himself to win this argument. He so much wanted to be left alone rather than rifle through his dad's things. Panda rolled his eyes. "*Might as well get it over with.*" With a stiff nod, Drew climbed back up the stairs and abandoned his bowl of chips in the kitchen. Reluctantly, he followed his mom into her room. She slid open the closet door to his dad's half. His nostrils caught the smell of his dad's cologne. His nose flared. His stomach tightened. His hands clenched. He was reminded of those awful words from earlier. "*Did Dad really think we're nothing?*" Panda echoed Drew's doubt.

His mom's cold hand on his arm jolted him back. Her worry crease weighed her brows down. Her lips pressed tightly. With a deep breath to steady herself, Celeste dove into the closet and held up a black and a dark navy blue suit. Drew was immediately stumped. There were too many options already. Panda pointed to the black one. Celeste carefully put the suit on the bed, and then returned the other one to the closet.

"Do you have a date?" she inquired, facing the closet.

"I do," Drew coughed out.

Celeste bit her tongue, trying to curb her enthusiasm. She didn't want to scare him off. This was already the most he'd talked to her without some underlying attitude. Drew felt out of place in his parents' room. He was disturbing the peaceful rest of their closet. "Do you know what her color is?"

"She said purple." His mom turned to him with patience. Shrugging, he said, "But like a 'periwinkle' purple? Whatever that is." He choked on a laugh. Panda remembered their conversation with Miranda. Her friends were going for a purple theme. It was crucial everyone stuck to their specific shade.

Celeste snickered with him. She took a step back and took in his dad's wardrobe with her arms crossed. She tilted her head as she eyeballed the closet. "I've got an idea."

She reached in and pulled out a white button up shirt and a black vest. From a drawer, she withdrew a handful of ties. Drew had forgotten about his father's lavish attire. When he wasn't in camouflage or roughing it in the backyard in jeans, his dad would treat his mother out to a night of dancing and fancy dinners. Drew felt immediately drawn to a pale purple tie with intricate black filigree. Seeing which one caught her son's attention, she removed the purple one and added it to the pile.

"Go ahead," her chin jutted toward her restroom.

Drew stared at the bathroom. His nerves were starting to get the best of him. "*This is wrong. What if they don't fit? What if they do fit? Would Dad be ok with this? Do we have a right to rummage through his stuff?*" Celeste took a step forward. Despite her gentle hands on his shoulders, he still winced at the touch.

"You know how much he wishes he were here, right?"

Her dark eyes were pleading. Normally, Drew hated that look. It stank of pity. Desperation. A mournful want to reconnect, like she wanted to make her child whole again. He hadn't been whole since he was thirteen. His dad dying last year hadn't helped things. But today, that look, of all looks, made his eyes sting. "*Maybe Mom is right…*"

Drew nodded his head and breathed out a low-spirited, "Yeah." He grabbed the clothes and shuffled to the bathroom.

He refused to look at his reflection as he changed. It was weird enough that he was borrowing his dead dad's clothes. The fabric still smelled like his cologne and aftershave, threatening to choke Drew as he buttoned the top of his shirt. He expected his scars to retaliate against the material. But the smooth fabric calmed his scorching marks. He stared down at the tie, unsure of how to put it on.

Suddenly, Drew found himself lost in a memory, and Panda let him wander through it in his mind…

Drew was 10. It was cold that night, a kind of freezing that splintered the bones. There wasn't enough moisture in the air to snow. The army base was holding a winter banquet and his dad really had no interest in going, but his mom wanted to show him support and spend some time with the other wives. Her belly was swollen with Evie and his dad aimed to please her. If she wanted to go somewhere else for the evening, he wouldn't have hesitated.

A teenage girl in the neighborhood was coming over to babysit Drew. She hadn't arrived yet. Jamie had looked after him for years until she graduated high school. She made him either pizza or mac and cheese and shared some of her soda with him. She even gave him full TV rights. Dark freckles speckled her face and her braces looked like a barbed-wire trap. Her hair was always in a ponytail and she wore ripped jeans and a t-shirt. Drew liked that she was so nice to him.

Young Drew watched his dad get ready in his habitual, methodical way. He would iron his clothes with measured movements. Drew could hear the hiss of the iron, clear as day. Then, his dad would shave until his face was smooth, shower, and then apply aftershave. He'd splash some cologne on his bare skin before he got dressed. It was odd how his dad would put his shoes on first, and then his pants, with everything else following. His tie was always last.

Drew would sit still as a board as his dad wrapped the tie around Drew's neck. The soft fabric gently brushed his neck and face as his dad tied the knot. Once finished, the tie would be loosened and gently pulled over Drew's head. Then it went over his dad's head and was secured around his neck. Last, he would turn his collar down. After he was dressed, his dad always struck a pose for Drew, waiting for the seal of approval. Drew would constantly give him one with a thumbs up.

Drew felt tears well up in his eyes. He could remember

what his dad was really like. Loving. Kind. Playful. Patient. Strong. He was stern when he needed to be. But fair. His father was his goddamned hero. And Drew felt like he was drowning, failing at being his son. "I miss him so much…" he whispered before a knock at the door tore the happy memory away.

"Drew?"

He couldn't answer his mom. Finally, looking up at his reflection, Drew's breath caught in his throat. He felt like he couldn't breathe. He didn't know how to feel about wearing his dad's clothes. Sure, he was borrowing them, but he couldn't ask his dad for permission. He felt like he had no right wearing these clothes. These were the clothes that his dad used to take his mom out to dinners in and schmooze his old colleagues in. In his reflection, Drew could see the similarities he shared with his father. They were written all over his DNA.

Drew didn't want to admit how well the clothes fit him. His brown eyes and curly hair were from his mom. But he had his dad's pointed chin and round ears. If he looked straight on at his nose, it was slightly pudgy like his mom. But when he turned his face to look at his profile, the angle of his nose was sharp like his dad's. Drew's forehead was square like his dad's, too. He'd never look exactly like his father in the same sense that Liam did, but wearing his clothes and seeing how he was an extension of his dad was all too much to handle.

Drew struggled to take in air and crumpled to the floor in a heap. He inhaled sharply, trying to keep his sobs quiet. Panda sat solemnly on the edge of the bathtub, hesitant in knowing how to console Drew. The door slowly creaked open. Celeste was unsure of what state of decency her son was in. She found him on the floor. His hands covered his face and he was sniffling hard into his hands. Panda tried to wave their mom away and tell her to go away. But Drew couldn't move. Couldn't speak. The grief hit him like a freight train. It felt like it hit harder since he had never let himself cry like this before.

Drew stilled as he felt Celeste sit beside him. She instinctively wrapped her arm over his shoulders. For the first time in years, he melted into her arms. She held him tight against her chest as he shuddered against her, sobbing roughly. He could feel her trembling against him as she cried alongside him. After a moment, he felt her hand rubbing his back. Drew could finally feel all of it.

CHAPTER FIFTEEN

"*Liking the drip, dude!*" Panda threw up a thumb in approval and straightened out his own bright-pink bow tie. Panda was dressed immaculately in a pressed tuxedo.

Suppressing a retort at Panda's approval, Drew smoothed down his coat. He was still annoyed with him over their fight yesterday. But he wasn't going to bring it up tonight. This was going to be a good night. He looked back and forth between himself and Panda in the mirror. Drew still needed his mom to put his tie on. Other than that, he did look pretty sharp. Celeste had given him a haircut yesterday after he managed to calm himself. His kinky curls were now a manageable buzz cut and his short hair easily smoothed down with a course brush. He admired the slight fade his mom was able to give him on the sides. Drew realized how he had echoed his dad's dressing ritual.

First, he had attempted to iron out the clothes hanger bump on the pants and flatten out the sleeves that had been folded slightly after the shirt's deep slumber in the closet, all the while ignoring Panda's unreasonable fear that Drew would set the clothes on fire. Then he trimmed his facial hair. Panda was worried that Drew would cut himself, which caused Drew to concentrate so hard, he broke out in a sweat. A small tuft of curls still claimed his chin. Drew thought the small amount of facial hair made him look older somehow. The hot water of his shower burned his skin, but Drew allowed the water to heat up his soul and quiet his nerves for the upcoming evening. Afterwards, he used his dad's aftershave and cologne, applying just a small amount to his skin. He finally understood why his dad put his shoes on first as he got dressed. Panda was quick to point out the wrinkle Drew caused in the knees as he tied his shoes.

"*You can't ignore me forever,*" Panda's voice snapped Drew out of recounting every detail of his dressing ritual. Panda licked his finger then pressed it against his brow, attempting to smooth down the wispy fur.

"I'm still mad at you."

"*Be mad all you want. You'd only be mad at yourself.*" Panda chuckled to himself.

Drew scowled as he considered the fact that Panda might be right. He'd replayed their fight over and over in his head with what Panda had told him—that he could control Panda if he just believed in himself more. And that he really did have the power to be better.

"*Now,*" Panda clapped his hands together, "*don't worry about anything. It's going to be a great night.*" Then he gripped Drew's shoulders tightly like Drew was a boxer readying himself to enter the ring of social interaction. It was hellish trying to clear his mind to just get dressed. Drew felt a swirl of mixed emotions—pride in himself when he got ready, as if his dad were with him, encouraging him along the way, and grief as he struggled with his imposter syndrome. Drew couldn't think of any time Panda had just given him the night off.

"DREW!" his name echoed down the stairs.

Panda grumbled under his breath. Drew hurriedly stuffed his pockets with his phone, wallet, and keys. He grabbed his dad's tie off his nightstand and then paused. His eyes snapped over to his backpack. There were only a few grams of uppers left. Another successful night last night had brought him closer to ending things with Omar. Drew had worked his butt off unloading most everything in one week. Luckily, with Finals Week and summer vacation ahead, customers were needy. Could he really sell off the rest at his high school prom? *"Best to grab it just in case."* Panda thought. He stuffed the remaining handful of small bags in his other pocket. Hearing his name again, he hurriedly climbed up the stairs.

"Dude!" Trey greeted him first and then grabbed Drew tightly in a bear hug.

Drew's eyes wandered through the collective bodies gathered just outside the kitchen. Trey was basically a copy of Drew, except for the dark purple bow tie. Drew's eyes paused on Wynter. His heart fluttered. *"Look at that sparkling dress!"* Panda exclaimed. Each time Wynter's body shifted, it captivated Drew's attention. The sparkles on her black dress were like a million tiny camera flashes when different angles of light caught them. He would've been surprised at the girlish effect, but was comforted to see that Wynter stuck with her normal style of black manicured nails and a black dress.

The dress hugged her hourglass figure tightly. Spaghetti straps held firmly on her narrow shoulders. Her plump lips were a glossy burgundy. Seductive silvery eyes popped from her smoky eye shadow. Wynter had straightened her hair.

Drew couldn't remember the last time he saw her hair straightened. *"Maybe middle school?"* But it was in a large bun on top of her head. Strands curled with purpose framed her round face. Her familiar choker with the emerald gem stood out against her dark skin.

Evie's surprised gasp made Drew's grin spread even wider. "You look handsome," she complimented.

He bent down and picked her up, not caring about the wrinkles that were slowly taking form around his waist. "Thanks, Eves."

"Yes, you do," Celeste agreed, almost tearfully. She gingerly gripped his shoulder.

"Hmm," the sound came deep from Liam's throat. "I guess you kind of look like my brother." Panda bristled at this. Drew's stomach dropped as he took in Liam. Drew was old enough to remember how his dad was and what he looked like. Thankfully he recognized enough differences between the twins. But Liam's comment twisted at Drew's insides.

"You missed a spot," Liam criticized as he pointed to Drew's chin, referencing the small cleft of facial hair. Drew felt instantly self-conscious of it now. "You need help with that tie, dude?" Liam gestured to the tie in Drew's hand.

"No." Drew tried to curb the venom in Panda's voice.

He put Evie down and stood in front of his mom, silently asking her to tie it for him. He passed the satin material to her. Her eyes shone as she happily did this for her son. The only way he could enjoy this night was knowing his mom had the night off to watch Evie. She wasn't on-call either. He wondered if she had pre-planned it like that.

"You do look like him," Celeste gripped his face when the satin material was tied securely. "And I know just how proud of you he is."

Drew blinked furiously. Ignoring his own doubt, he focused on what his mom said, trying to dislodge Liam's comment.

"Ready?" Trey slapped him on the back.

"Yeah," Drew half smiled.

"Oh!" Celeste wiped her tears away, suddenly jolted with purpose. She scrambled for her phone. "Let me get some pictures!" The three of them indulged his mom as she took a zillion photos. To Drew's shock, it was Liam who started shoving them out the house.

Trey drove them to Miranda's. Wynter was un-characteristically quiet in the back. Panda could sense her irritation emanating the closer they got to Miranda's. Drew figured she was reciting her "If you don't have anything nice to say, don't say anything at all" mantra. He appreciated his friend's sacrifice. "*Sydney Porter will be there no doubt...*" Panda reminded. Along with a handful of other cheerleaders and their dates... Drew finished Panda's thought in his mind. Given the history of Porter and Wynter, this part of the evening was bound to be awkward. Drew still couldn't believe that Trey and Porter had broken up.

After that night when Trey acted as Drew's getaway driver, Drew had thought about their relationship some more. He was proud of his friend for breaking up with Porter. She was toxic and controlling. Drew was just relieved to have his best friend back. Panda made Drew feel guilty for immediately finding joy in his friend's misfortune. But Trey seemed unaffected by the whole ordeal. All the same, Drew remembered how devastated Trey was after that Sunday night. Drew thought Trey probably didn't want to dwell on it in front of his friends who weren't exactly Sydney Porter supporters.

Besides, Miranda was still Drew's date and he wanted to have his cake and eat it too. He wanted to go to prom with Miranda AND his two best friends.

As Panda predicted, it was awkward. Luckily, the manic

energy of Mrs. Goodman and three other moms kept things moving. Encircled by Wynter and a handful of the school's jocks, Drew watched with nervous anticipation as the clique of girls descended the stairs. Sydney and Trey still matched with their shades of purple. But Trey didn't seem fazed by it at all. *"Unlike Porter."* Panda wanted to laugh seeing how unhappy Sydney was. She kept throwing Trey hateful glares as he pretended to ignore her. Unsurprisingly, she had managed to find herself another date on such short notice. *"Obviously a rebound. Poor Devón!"* Drew sympathized with Panda on that one.

Trey was more than happy to go as Wynter's date even though Wynter didn't care. She was fine flying solo. Trey might have felt guilty about Porter's actions, or maybe he didn't want to go solo. Either way, Wynter obliged him. "We're just going as friends," Trey had reassured Drew earlier that week with an elbow shove. Drew didn't want to look into it further because he couldn't explain his conflicted feelings. All he knew was that he somehow felt better knowing they were going as "friends."

Miranda came down the stairs last. Evie would have called her a princess if she'd seen her. Miranda blushed as she locked eyes with Drew. He noted how her blueish, or purplish dress, *"it's periwinkle,"* Panda corrected, wrapped snuggly around the top and then fanned at her waist. White lace flowers adorned her gown at the top in close clusters and then thinned toward the bottom. Her chocolate waves were curled even more, with a section pinned back behind her right ear. Elongated lashes threatened to blow Drew down with each blink. As she made her way to the bottom of the stairs and stood in front of him, Drew smelled the divine scent of strawberries. They exchanged shy hellos while the room swarmed with more conversation.

Drew placed his nervous hands on her waist as the moms took photographs. Then they all moved out to the front of the house, taking another zillion photos. *"Interior and exterior. I want to die! Can we get going already?! I wanna show off my dance moves!"* Panda whined from the sidelines, dancing like he had a Hula-Hoop around his narrow waist.

Miranda's smooth, creamy skin blushed even more when Drew managed to whisper in her ear, "You look beautiful."

When the group of teenagers finally managed to escape the overprotective mothers, they drove downtown in four separate vehicles. Wynter sat up front with Trey and attempted to distract herself from Miranda's presence by chatting with Trey. Her smoky eyes flicked to the back from time to time, aware of how comfortable Drew and Miranda were together. They seemed to be in their own little world. The sun had finally set. The bright glow of the streetlights passed by in a soothing rhythm. Miranda sat close to Drew, burying her face deep in his neck. They whispered compliments back and forth, sometimes exchanging giggles.

Drew felt brave for a moment and pulled her in closer. He gripped her bare shoulder with his arm across her back keeping her in place. "*SMOOTH!*" Panda praised him.

The four entered the building in awe. The student council had managed to transform the stuffy ballroom where the dance was being held into a spectacular display of white streamers, balloons, and shimmering lights. Drew couldn't quite explain what magical powers Miranda had. But when he was with her, he seemed lighter.

After taking it all in, they made their way to the dance floor, dancing as a group for a bit until a slow song came on. Drew took Miranda into his arms and as she formed her body to his, Panda's random, intrusive thoughts still managed to leak through, "*Grab her butt!*" and "*Is now a good time for a boner?*" Drew shushed Panda and noticed that as Miranda danced with him, his buzzing skin was quiet. His abusive thoughts were silent. His heart was tranquil. There wasn't his fear for Evie that usually kept him on edge. Drew realized he could allow himself to relax and be present with his friends and Miranda. He could just enjoy this time with them.

Miranda occasionally danced with her friends for a song or two, which gave Drew a break to mingle with Trey and Wynter. To assuage his stress about Omar, he managed to sell more than half the remaining bags in his pocket when he told his friends he was going to the bathroom. These were regulars who'd assumed Drew would be carrying. "*Careful!*" Panda cautioned. "*Make sure Miranda's not looking. Just because she knows we're a drug dealer doesn't mean she has to see it.*"

As he came back to the ballroom, Drew discretely pocketed the money and leaned against the wall at the edge of the ballroom, shrouded in the shadows. He found himself looking at Wynter too long and suddenly felt an ache in his heart to reach out to her. Panda urged him on, "*We can't let her be mad at us. We're running out of time! She's going to be in France next year! FIX THIS.*" Drew agreed with Panda. He felt terrible he hadn't defended Wynter like Trey had. But Drew wasn't ready to confront the one girl who liked him in return.

A slow song came on just as Miranda skipped out for

some fresh air with Porter and the others. Drew looked at Wynter again. Her arms were crossed and her face was pinched as she looked around. Drew looked around too. Everyone in the ballroom was already paired off. Trey was nowhere to be seen. *"He probably found a girl to occupy his night!"* Panda scoffed. Drew only knew that Wynter was alone at this moment. He strolled toward her with confident steps.

"May I hov dess danse, mah chere?" he asked in a terrible French accent, holding his hand out. His other hand clutched at his heart dramatically.

Wynter choked on a laugh, *"Oui, monsieur."*

Drew held her closely as Cults "Always Forever" swirled around them. Taking a deep breath, Wynter placed her head against his shoulder. *"She smells nice."* Panda hummed in bliss. They swayed in a peaceful slow circle. Panda couldn't help pointing out the differences between Wynter and Miranda. *"Wynter is softer. A little taller too. They both smell amazing. Wynter like almonds and coconut. Miranda like strawberries. Both of their eyes are stunning. Miranda with her bright, brown eyes. Wynter and her rare, grey eyes. Miranda's lips are thinner, with a cupid's bow. Wynter's are fuller."*

"You look beautiful tonight," Drew abruptly announced.

She snorted with disbelief, "Thanks."

"No, really."

Wynter shook her head. "It's the dress."

"It's you," Panda blurted out before Drew could stop him.

He didn't disagree. Wynter quickly became quiet. She pulled away and her wide eyes searched his face. They eventually stopped their half circle and stood still. Drew embraced her in a close hug.

"I'm going to miss you."

She held him tighter, "I'm not going anywhere."

"Well, you are," Drew started.

Wynter interrupted him with a small laugh. She pulled back again to look at him. "Nobody is going to drive a wedge, Drew. You're my best friend." Wynter shyly shrugged a shoulder.

Panda calmed back down. Gratified with her response, Drew gave her a crooked smile. "You're my best friend too." This earned him a blush from her. Wynter opened her mouth to say something else. Panda was entirely too focused on the fullness of her lips. The corners of her mouth twitched, trying to get her thoughts out.

"What is it?" Drew coaxed.

"Drew…" she took a shaky breath. "I…" she turned her head. Her eyes widened in mortification. She clamped her mouth closed and took a forceful step back from Drew.

His arms felt like they had been ripped off him and his body felt cold from her withdrawal. Drew's eyes crinkled in confusion. His chest constricted at her quick movement. "*What happened?*" Panda was quick to blame.

Wynter offered a small smile and cleared her throat. "*That smile is fake,*" Panda confirmed. Drew followed her line of sight. Miranda was watching them carefully, a little stunned.

"Uh, Miranda…" Drew took a step forward toward his date, and then paused. He literally felt like he was being torn in half as he looked back at his best friend.

"It's ok," Wynter hurriedly said. "You should finish the song with her."

Drew's body twitched. He was unsure of which direction to go in. Wynter's lips pressed into a tight smile. She took another step back, making the decision for Drew.

"I'll catch you later. Yeah?" Drew consoled with a thick voice. Wynter hurriedly nodded then turned on her heel and left the dance floor, missing Drew's pained expression. "*Miranda's waiting…*" Panda reminded him. "*Decide. Wynter is our best friend. But you came to the dance with Miranda.*" Drew cleared his throat and turned to face Miranda with a gentle smile. Miranda softened in his arms as Drew finished the slow song with her.

CHAPTER SIXTEEN

"Drew! Drew!" Evie shouted as she launched herself halfway up his bed with animated jumps.

Panda groaned at the sudden assault. "What?"

"Last day of school! Uncle Liam's making pancakes." She snickered like a maniac.

"*We're not eating his pancakes!*" Panda scoffed. "Eves," Drew rolled over to look at her, "can you put some Pop Tarts in the toaster for me?"

"But pancakes…" her eyes darted behind Drew for a moment.

The confused look on her face just about killed him. "More for you, right?" Drew poked at her sides a few times, attempting to lighten her mood.

She tried to resist but was unable to contain her giggles

for long. "Uncle Liam said it's time to get up."

Panda and Drew collectively sighed. "Alright. Give me a minute." Drew half chuckled when he heard her excited feet depart. Hollow footsteps reverberated through the ceiling and echoed down into Drew's room.

"*We should skip,*" Panda persuaded.

"How much do you wanna bet she'll forget the Pop Tarts?" Drew ignored him as he got out of bed. He tried to get ready quickly, but Panda wasn't a morning person, so Drew's body moved groggily.

"*Why can't we skip?*"

"I need my report card."

Panda groaned dramatically. "*Let me guess, a C in every-thing.*" With a sneer he said, "*I can hear Celeste's disapproval now.*" Panda stared at Drew. But Drew didn't respond. He just wandered around his room, slowly getting dressed.

Panda pulled the sheets up over his chest. Striking a sexy pose, he propped his head up by his hand and ogled Drew. "*Last day of school. What to wear?*" Drew pulled on his normal black jeans. "*Black! Excellent choice, darling. And shirt?*"

"Whatever's clean," Drew shrugged. He was already tired of Panda's dramatics for the day.

Drew picked up random shirts on the floor, smelling each

one for its level of cleanliness. Thinking better of it, he went for a sure thing—a clean shirt in his drawer. Ignoring the millions of fold wrinkles, he pulled the red crew neck over his head. Panda dressed himself in a discarded shirt Drew had thrown back on the floor. After finishing the rest of his routine, Drew climbed up the stairs, Panda in tow.

"Hey dude," Liam greeted him too radiantly, busy at the sink. Drew ignored the salutation. He looked over at the empty toaster. Shuffling his feet, he put his breakfast in the slots and pressed down the lever. "Hey," Liam spoke lowly over his shoulder, "your mom just got in from her night shift, so keep it down, ok?"

Drew's stomach clenched. How long had Evie been up with Liam? When his breakfast popped up, he grabbed the hot rectangles and moved to sit by Evie. Who knew how many pancakes deep she already was in. That detail didn't matter. Drew watched his sister carefully. "*She seems fine,*" Panda assessed. Overjoyed with her breakfast, her head bobbed side to side. Liam sat down across from Drew. Panda mad dogged him while Drew ignored him, focused on his sister and his food.

Evie broke the awkward sound of scraping dishes and chewing. "Charlotte's got a sleepover tonight. Can I go?"

"Who's Charlotte?" Drew asked. He couldn't remember who this person was to Evie.

"She's in my class."

Evie looked at Drew for an answer, but Liam responded, "We should check with your mom." He winked at her over his mug.

She kicked her legs keenly and finished the last few bites on her plate. "Finished?" Panda asked a bit impatiently. He didn't want them in the house any longer. She nodded enthusiastically. "Go finish getting ready."

"My hair…" she started to whine, reaching her pudgy hands up to her head. Fuzzy wisps had managed to escape their ponytails and swayed slightly at the quick movement.

Drew snorted. "You have to get ready first." She urgently got off the chair and loudly began to rush to her room. "Be quiet for Mom," Drew reminded.

Her puttering quieted. Drew turned his head and found green eyes staring at him. His stomach dropped. How he hated that color. He especially hated how those eyes made him feel.

"You're really good with her. You know that?"

Drew bit back Panda's tongue. With a stiff nod, he grabbed Evie's dishes and took them to the sink. He started filling the dishwasher, avoiding further conversation with his uncle.

"So, summer starts tomorrow," Liam said as he grabbed his dishes. He paused next to Drew. "I figured you could have a week to yourself before starting at my shop."

A cold shiver ran up Drew's spine. His body froze, causing silverware to clatter loudly in the dishwasher.

"Hey, man, your mom's asleep," Liam's tone turned sharp. He set his dishes on the counter.

Drew stood up straighter and faced his uncle. "I'm not working for you."

Liam snapped his fingers at him, with a half-attempted chuckle. All earlier charm was out the window as his eyes turned cold. "Right…because you're making so much more money as a drug dealer."

"Better than being a dead-end mechanic," Drew threw back. Panda crossed his arms, standing behind Drew in support. "Don't think I've forgotten about that bullshit you pulled with my mom last week."

"Or what, big man?" Liam put his hands on his hips and leaned in closer.

Drew could smell the coffee on Liam's breath, but he refused to back down.

"Are you going to have your gang beat me up?"

"Can't have a gang if I'm not dealing anymore," Drew confidently lied. "*We only have a couple baggies of uppers left. We can for sure unload the rest today,*" Panda chimed in. "Besides, I don't need a gang to fight you."

Liam's lips spread into a smirk.

Drew cringed when he saw the delight on Liam's face.

With a tsk, Liam said, "I'm right here." His arms spread open, a silent invitation for Drew to take his best shot.

Panda's hands tightened into fists, ready to take Liam on. But Drew set his jaw. He kept his body still, fighting against Panda, as he stared his uncle down.

"Drew, I'm ready," Evie whisper-yelled behind him. Drew kept eye contact with Liam for half a second longer before he threw on a fake smile and turned to face his little sister.

Panda and Drew left Liam in the kitchen. Panda released the intense breath he was holding and Drew's body relaxed as he led Evie to the bathroom. He felt more at ease in his sister's presence, but only a little bit. He had to get them out of the house.

He rattled off the checklist, "Teeth brushed? Face washed? Bed made? Bag packed?" Evie nodded to every single one. Then she readily jumped up on the counter, and faced the mirror, ready for her hair to be done. Panda and Drew squished their cheeks next to hers. "Last day of school," Drew said. "We need to make a statement!" Panda sparkled.

She thought for a moment.

Drew mumbled inaudibly, "Please don't be caterpillars. Please don't be caterpillars."

"*You definitely need more practice, dude,*" Panda critiqued.

To both their relief, Evie replied, "Bunnies."

Drew squinted at her. "Up or down?"

"Down," she whispered, hiding her smile behind her hands.

"Down?"

Evie bobbed her head and Drew got to work on creating two, anti-frizz, ponytails. He loved this one. It was so easy to wet her hair with leave-in conditioner, smooth it down to her scalp with a course brush and a little gel, and then gently comb and tie her hair off into two pig tails. The final touch was scrunching her hair up with his damp hand. Afterwards, Evie's kinky curls bounced wildly with her enthusiasm.

Drew ran downstairs, finished getting ready, and quickly threw his backpack over his shoulder. On the way out the door, Evie high-fived her uncle and waved goodbye to her dad's photo for the day. Ignoring both figures, Drew followed, knowing this would be the last time he would walk her to school for the next two and a half months.

"Hey Eves?"

She didn't look up from the rock she kicked along. "Yeah?"

"If mom isn't home tonight, you can go to Charlotte's."

She nearly ripped his arm out of its socket from excitement. "Really?!"

He chuckled and nodded, giving her his consent again.

When they arrived at Evie's school, Drew held her by the shoulders. "I'll be here after school." "*Like always.*" Panda vowed. She held her pinkie out to him. He stood up and pinkie promised her. As he held onto her finger, he tapped the inside of his ankle with her ankle. After their ritual, she hugged him goodbye. "I promise."

"With Miranda?" Evie asked with the wiggle of her brow.

"Get inside," he attacked her sides. She screamed in laughter as he tickled her. Then he scooped her up and gave her a quick kiss on her cheek. Like releasing an animal into the wild, he watched her run inside the school.

Drew hated the last day of school. It just seemed like four

wasted hours of glorified babysitting. This year was different though. Panda was thrilled over Drew's grades. He managed to get a B in everything. Celeste would be proud. Especially compared to his C's last year. "*Last year was rough,*" Panda agreed.

Going to the end-of-year assembly wasn't such a drag this year. Maybe it was because Miranda was next to him. Although, he had to admit, watching the seniors inflate their egos and having to sit through all the awards was still a grind. Holding Miranda's hand made it all the much better. "*I know! Holy crap!*" Panda noticed that Sydney was seething at them a few rows over. Drew was thankful Miranda and Trey got along. He could tell Wynter was trying with Miranda. But her responses were clipped and short whenever Miranda tried talking to her. "*At least they are on speaking terms now.*"

The halls were packed after the assembly let out. Wide-open lockers exposed forgotten gym clothes to anyone who walked by. Drew cringed as he found a half-eaten sandwich at the bottom of his locker. Panda gagged, blocking his air passageways. "*How long has THAT been in here?*"

As Drew searched for a trash can, he saw lots of his classmates sprawled out on the floor, signing yearbooks. Only a handful of people had signed Drew's yearbook. He didn't really care about that kind of stuff, but he had to chuckle when Wynter claimed a whole page to herself. He took a deep breath as he waded through the chaotic wave of teenagers in the hallway. Loud chatter vibrated off the metal lockers. There were smiles as far as he could see and laughter echoed down every hall. As silly as it was to force them to show up to school for four hours, the air somehow felt different.

Optimistic.

Summer was just an hour away. Drew was one hour away from being a senior. And then he would be one step away from graduating, finally able to move out of that miserable hole he called home. A guilty, cold shiver crawled up his spine. Could he really leave Evie behind? *"Never mind. We're not thinking about THAT right now."* Panda immediately dismissed the depressing thought.

Miranda had busied herself with her friends. They agreed to meet up later to pick up their sisters from school. Trey was hanging out with his football buddies. They had agreed that Drew would show up early for his end-of-year party later that evening. And Wynter, in all her paranoid splendor, was confirming details about her exchange program with her counselor. Drew was used to being on his own. *"Now's the time.*" Panda urged him. "*Let's be done with this once and for all!*" Panda said, motioning his head toward Zac, who nearly bumped into Drew.

"Dude," Drew's tweaking classmate, Zac, said as he looked wildly around the hallway. They both noticed that teachers were hiding in their offices and security guards were just chatting with other students. No one was looking at them. "At school? Bit high-key, don't you think?" Zac asked in a frantic, suspicious whisper. "I don't need any more. I've still got the pills from prom." He looked like he was backing up.

"I'm retiring, Zac," Drew said to Zac's alarmed face. "This is it."

"No... What am I supposed to do?"

Drew shrugged indifferently, "Kurt's still in the game."

Zac waved his hand dismissively, "Kurt's a dick."

"Better than nothing. You want some or not?" This time Drew looked around to make sure they weren't being watched.

Zac sighed in desperation. "Yeah, ok. How much you got left?"

"You can have the rest for seventy bucks."

Zac looked offended. "What makes you think I got

seventy bucks?"

Drew cocked his head. He was not going to miss this aspect of it at all. "That's not my problem. Figure it out or kick rocks." Panda prayed, *"Please don't actually leave."*

Zac licked his lips and eyed the crowd closely. "Yo, let me find Vic."

Drew only had to wait ten minutes for Zac and his buddy, Victor, to approach him. Victor was another skinny, strung-out teenager. Whereas Zac was always a hyper twitching type, Victor was quieter and slower. He had huge dark rings under his eyes, like he could never sleep. Drew had to go through the painful rigmarole once again with Victor.

"But yo, why is it so expensive?" Victor drawled.

Drew shook his head with annoyance. "Because I'm taking all the risk, dumbass. You're pissing me off now, Vic. And wasting my fucking time. I'll give it to someone else. You think I care?" This time, Panda was ok if they lost the sale. A quick stop at the mall could set them free.

But impatience clawed at Drew. He turned to walk away, playing his bluff. He so wanted to be done.

"Wait," Zac held his hands up, barricading Drew against the wall. Drew sighed tiredly. He and Zac stared at Vic with expectation.

"Fine," Victor rolled his eyes with a groan.

As discretely as possible, they exchanged money and the remaining bags. Out the corner of Drew's eye, he saw one of the heavier set security guards making his way toward them. Drew stuffed the money in his pocket and hurriedly made his way out the building. He quickly shuffled his feet with his head down and his hands in his pockets, leaving a disgruntled Victor and an ecstatic Zac behind. His heart was pounding. Drew wasn't going to miss the close calls with authority either. Getting caught was the last thing he needed to kick start the summer. He'd never hear the end of it from his mom. Not missing his chance, he texted Omar.

DREW: Yo. Can we hang today?

Panda and Drew were more than happy to bail early. Leaving the school was easy. Staff really didn't care at that point where students went. Excited to graduate tomorrow, several seniors were loitering in the parking lot, reminiscing over their peak years. Drew walked past them with a pep in his step. Part of him used to dread the summer. It meant two and half months trying to distract himself, and watching Evie was a full-time job. But the prospect of spending time with Miranda and bringing Evie along eased his nerves. Plus, hopefully after tonight, he would finally be free of Omar. He knew that his financial independence would cease to exist for a while. That is, until he found a real job. Mainly, he was looking forward to being more available for his sister.

The weather was perfect as Drew walked home. It was right in that delicate window before it got too hot in the summer and was still not too cold as the end of spring neared. Drew looked up. The sky was an uncanny, bright blue. The clouds looked like brush strokes, contrasting with the superb green of the trees. Birds sang to him. Doubting his good mood, Drew looked over to Panda who was practically skipping beside him.

"*Relax.*" Panda whistled a tune that would eventually get stuck in Drew's head. "*Today is surprisingly a good day.*"

Suppressing a wry smile, Drew enjoyed the serenity for a moment. He walked through his front door. Pausing a moment, he didn't hear anything. He thought Liam was probably at work and his mom might still be sleeping. He wasn't about to check for either of them. He was just happy to have a quiet house to himself. He chanced a glance at his dad's shrine. The smile that looked tight four days ago looked soft now. Tender. Accepting.

"Hey Dad," Drew whispered.

This was the first time Drew had spoken to his dad in a

while. The pressure in his chest eased some. He took an uneven breath and fought the small tug on the corner of his mouth as he strode to the kitchen and rummaged through the fridge and cupboards like a raccoon.

The sounds of faint giggles raced up his spine.

"*What was that?*" Panda whipped his head around, peering down the hallway.

Drew and Panda stared down the narrow hall for a moment, unsure of what to do next. The noise trickled down the hall again, causing goosebumps to race up Drew's arms. He didn't know who was making that noise. Instinctively, he grabbed the frying pan off the drying rack. Panda caused Drew's heart to beat erratically.

The pair silently crept down the hall, following the girlish laugh, which increased in volume the closer they got. Drew's hand rested on his mom's doorknob. Was that his mom? Laughing?

"*Umm…should we maybe…*" Panda started. For once, it was Panda who thought this was a bad idea. But it was too late. Drew's hand was already in motion. The door swung inward, eager to reveal the truth it concealed inside. Drew's hand was tight on the pan, ready for anything.

His mom yelped and clutched the sheets up to her throat

to cover her dark, bare skin. Drew didn't notice her indecent nature. Instead, red clouded his vision. Horror seized his body, gluing his feet to the floor. *"This can't be happening!"* Panda shouted from behind him. *"THIS CANNOT BE HAPPENING!"* Drew's head turned to see his father's revolting twin standing beside the bed in a pair of boxers, as if he was just returning to the bed from the bathroom. Edgy, green eyes stared widely at him and Liam held his hands up in defense.

"Drew!" Celeste called out in shock. *"You think she'd be angry. Her teenage son just barged into her room!"* She wasn't angry though. Her pitch was stunned by the fact that they had been caught. "Drew," she reached around for her robe, "let me explain."

Drew choked on a compulsory laugh. "You've got to be kidding me! Yes! Please explain away how you're sleeping with my uncle?" Scrutinizing eyes flashed to his mother. "Or is that not how it looks?"

"Don't talk to your mom like that," Liam took a step toward him.

"You can cut the bullshit with me, you dick!" Panda threatened. "You couldn't help yourself. Could you?"

"Drew," Celeste's tone sharpened. She was standing

now, covered in her robe.

Liam stood up straighter. "We don't have to explain ourselves to you, Drew. Your mom is a grown woman."

"What the fuck is wrong with you?" Drew pointed the pan at Liam.

"Drew!" His mom shouted at him. "Put that thing down."

"And what is wrong with YOU?" Drew turned his anger to his mom. He threw the pan on the floor, watching as it bounced slightly from the force. "He's not Dad! That's just sick!"

Celeste gasped at Drew's cruel words.

Drew turned to his father's twin, his mouth curled in a snarl. "How dare you fuck my mom! My dad did not die just so you could sleep with his wife!" Panda took control of Drew's arms and sharply thrust Liam backwards.

Liam shoved Drew back forcefully. "You need to back up right now, Drew." His muscles were as tight as his voice.

His mom strained to separate them. "Drew, let's go talk about this."

In one sudden and fluid motion, Drew's fist connected with Liam's jaw, hard. But Liam barely flinched at the punch. "*Which one of us did that?*" Panda asked in alarm. Sneering, Liam struck Drew back in the nose with a lightning-fast punch. Drew didn't see it coming, and his head snapped back from the blow. He staggered backwards a few steps then dropped to one knee.

"Hey!" Celeste stood in front of her son, defending him. "That's enough! Don't hit my son!"

It was too late. Drew was completely possessed. Panda's rage drove his limbs to stand up. He leapt around his mom, and dove into Liam's abdomen. Liam scraped his leg along the corner of the nightstand. He growled at the pain. Panda pinned him against the wall. Liam tried to break free, grabbing at Drew's shirt for leverage. He landed a few punches in Drew's side.

Drew's ribs screamed in protest. But Drew kept fighting alongside Panda, swinging his arms out. They hit Liam a few times in his side. Celeste's protests were muffled. Ignored. The lampshade on the nightstand crashed to the floor along with a pile of random remotes and books. Liam managed to hook his arm under Drew's right arm, lift him up slightly, and push him back again strongly. Drew's feet tangled together and he tripped over the bunched-up carpet and lampshade. Throwing his hands out, he barely caught his face from hitting the floor. Panda had Drew back on his feet once more. Liam was ready to throw another punch at his nephew.

"STOP!" Celeste screamed, getting between them. She held her hands out, hoping the measly barrier was enough to stop the fight.

Drew looked past his mother, nose flared, neck strained, lungs burning, sides aching. He stared back at his huffing uncle and adjusted his shirt. He was oblivious to the emotions on his mom's face, a swirl of shame, embarrassment, anger, and grief.

"Drew," she sighed trying to gather her words, "please…can we talk about this?"

Her words hung in the air. The house grew still. Liam's huffing hushed. Nothing in the house dared to make a noise.

Panda wanted to intervene, but Drew was so focused on what was in front of him that he didn't need Panda to step in. Drew's eyes squinted slightly as he looked at his mom, "I'm done talking." He picked his eyes up and addressed his uncle, "Am I supposed to be grateful you went after my mom and not Evie? You sick, son-of-a-bitch!"

"Drew, it's not like that." Liam's hands relaxed and he held them up in surrender.

"I didn't think you liked them older than eighteen. Or women for that matter. Should you tell her, or should I?"

Drew challenged.

Liam's back straightened. His eyes widened as he picked up on Drew's threat. "I'm trying to be better." His jaw was tight.

Celeste looked between the two of them. "What is he talking about? WHAT is going on?" Celeste was on the verge of yelling again.

Drew nearly coughed from disbelief. "And sleeping with my mom is better? Your dead brother's wife?! Do you think that's what he meant by 'take care of her'?" Drew's stomach churned at the thought of his uncle having sex with his mom. The image was enough to send him into another stupor of rage.

"Celeste," Liam tried to change directions, but it was too late.

For the second time, Drew didn't know if it was him or Panda. But something within him broke. In this vulnerable second, he was done carrying the weight of a grown man's secret. He was tired of all the guilt and burden. The shame ate away at him every day! He was tired reliving the worst day of his life. His flesh was burning. His scars were screaming for attention, edging him to do it. Drew pulled his shirt up and the waistband of his jeans down just a little bit, revealing three diligently placed scars. Numbers fifteen, sixteen, and seventeen.

Celeste gasped. She placed a hand over her mouth.

Without flinching, Drew looked at his mom. "Did he tell you he touched me?" Drew snorted. He tried to suppress the anger, fear, and immense vulnerability that clawed at his throat. "Did you know that I cut myself to get over how he abused me? That he's really a fucking pedophile?!"

Drew pulled his shirt back down and stormed out of the bedroom. High-pitched ringing pierced his ears. He couldn't hear his mom calling after him or her screaming at Liam to explain himself. He didn't hear Liam's fumbling excuses.

Drew ran to the garage. He grabbed his bike and made his escape.

His nose pulsed. His heart beat madly. A blood mustache took form. His skin hummed against his clothes. He could feel a solid brick inside his stomach. His sweaty, sore hands gripped the handlebars for dear life, turning his knuckles white from the tension. He kept pumping his legs to keep them from shaking. He inhaled unstable breaths as his ribs protested. He disregarded the musical ringtone of his phone as it went off every 30 seconds.

Drew didn't know how long he biked for. Even if he

wanted to go be with his friends right now, they were all busy. Besides, he wasn't in the mood to explain what the hell just happened. Panda kept pace with Drew on his skateboard, totally silent for once. Drew biked further, north of town to a popular picnic and hiking area. He found a lone tree at the park and threw his bike down, taking shelter under the shade. He heaved for air as he relived the confrontation again and again in his head.

"*Can I say something?*" Panda started, his tone even.

Drew shrugged. He knew Panda would tell him regardless of what his answer was. Panda picked at the grass, squinting as he looked over the park.

"*I'm proud of you.*"

Drew snorted. Tasting blood, he dislodged the crimson snot. "Proud of me for punching my uncle?"

"*Proud of you for fighting back against your abuser.*"

Drew sucked on his teeth. He stiffly nodded and leaned back against the tree. Now he just needed to reign his adrenaline in from the edge of the cliff. A gentle breeze brushed at his arms. He sat there and watched lazy clouds roll by until it was time to head over to Miranda's. Birds occasionally tweeted back and forth. He could hear a dog barking a block over. His phone rang in intervals.

CHAPTER SEVENTEEN

The constant notification chimes on Drew's phone became soothing after a while. As he waited for Miranda to open the door, Drew decided it would be best to text Celeste. "*Just one,*" Panda advised. Drew looked at and brushed off Liam's three threatening texts, ignored the thirty-two missed calls from his mom, and scrolled through the nineteen texts from her. He sent her one lone message.

DREW: I'm picking up Evie

"Oh my God," Miranda's smile dropped as soon as she opened her front door. "What happened to your face?"

Drew returned the now silent phone to his back pocket. He placed his hands in his front pockets and took a breath, "I...got into it with my uncle."

"Oh my God," she repeated. She took a step forward,

carefully cradling his face as she looked intensely at him, inspecting his injuries. His eyes softened as she went into care mode for him. "Are you ok? What happened?" She shifted his head slightly.

"Can we actually…" Drew shook his head a little, causing her hands to loosen a bit. Looking down, he rocked slightly up and down on the balls of his feet, "…not talk about it. I'm ok though. Really." He held her hands in place and picked his eyes up. Her attention snapped to his eyes. Her eyes shone with concern.

Miranda nodded. "Let's clean you up before getting the girls." She grabbed his hand and led him inside, shoved him into the guest bathroom, and quickly followed. "*She probably wants to avoid Mrs. Goodman seeing us like this.*" Drew let her carefully dab at his upper lip. Panda felt like a baby being cleaned like that. Drew paid attention to the crease she got between her brows when she concentrated.

"You got a few drops of blood on your shirt," she half said to herself. "Good call on wearing red today." She turned away from him.

Drew stood up of his own volition and bit the inside of his cheek. Panda was surprised by Drew's initiative. Drew's stomach flip-flopped with his determination. He wanted to reach out to Panda for comfort and reassurance for his actions, but he didn't. Instead, Drew charged on. He decided he had to do this himself.

Focused on the sink, Miranda rinsed the blood from the washcloth. She didn't notice him move closer. Maybe it was bravery, adrenaline, or stupidity, but Drew finally found the courage he had lacked on prom night. In the final inning, he had choked. He had walked her to her door, but became a heaving, embarrassed mess, suddenly too shy to make his move. That was in the past. In this moment, Drew felt empowered that anything can happen in life. He was ready to take a chance.

He placed a hand on Miranda's hip. Her movements stilled. She was aware of how close he was to her. Sucking in a deep breath, she turned to face him. She could smell his cologne and feel the counter pressed solidly behind her. His eyes darkened with longing as he stared down at her. He was wary not to do anything she wasn't comfortable with, despite Panda chanting *"DO IT! DO IT! DO IT!"* right in his ear.

Miranda took another shaky breath, but not out of distress. Did she really want this as badly as he did? When her eyes flicked down to his full lips, she nodded ever so slightly. Slowly, so slowly, he leaned down until his lips connected with her glossy ones. Panda clapped joyfully, perched on the toilet. As soon as their lips touched, Drew's nose pressed firmly into her cheek. He hissed sharply.

Miranda pulled back with a loud smack. "I'm sorry!" She grabbed at his face forcefully. Checking to make sure it didn't start bleeding again.

Drew chuckled deep in his throat. "You're fine."

He held her hands to his face. Huffing under her breath, she stretched up on her toes. Puckering her lips in exaggeration. With an amused snort, he leaned forward, careful of his nose, and gave her a quick peck. Not exactly how he imagined his first kiss. With a bloody nose, bruised face, in a bathroom. But it was still nice sharing it with Miranda. Drew felt like he was checking off boxes.

Go to prom…check!

Have your first kiss…check!

With any luck he could check off getting his driver's permit this summer. Drew quickly looked over to Panda. The furry humanoid gave him a thumbs up, but didn't seem as excited as he was before. Drew pressed his lips into a thin line. He expected Panda to be thrilled about this development between him and Miranda. Why wasn't he more animated?

Leaning back, Miranda sported a lazy smile. "I've got a spare shirt if you want to borrow it?" She jabbed her thumb toward the stairs on the other side of the door.

Drew looked down at his collar. "*You can barely tell.*" Panda reassured. Drew dismissed the stain on his shirt, "I'm good. Thanks."

Miranda bobbed her head once. "Ok. Let's go get the girls."

She opened the bathroom door and pulled Drew along by the hand. He released a heavy breath as they went out the front door. Their fingers interlocked as they walked to the school. Drew happily let Miranda talk the whole way. She kept his mind from wondering about what waited for him and Evie at home.

They both saw Evie come out first. Miranda stepped a few feet away to get a better look at the door for Maddison. Evie ran up to Drew with uncontainable excitement. He knelt down, catching her before she crashed into him. Her gap-toothed smile dropped as she saw his face upon closer inspection.

"*Shit! Your face, dude.*" Drew didn't even consider Evie would notice. He didn't think it was that bad. "*Dude, your nose is all sorts of bruised,*" Panda winced.

Evie's chubby hands grabbed his cheeks forcefully. He tried not to wince at her grip. Her light brown eyes were wide as she asked, "What happened?"

Drew cringed at her loud question. "Don't worry about it," he answered.

"Who hurt you?" Evie pressed. Her observant eyes noticed the blood on his shirt. Her eyes flickered to Drew's left where Panda was standing. Panda's blood went cold as he made eye contact with Evie. "*Did she just look at me?!*" Panda shrieked.

Evie looked back to Drew. "Who hurt you? Did he hurt you?"

Not knowing who she was talking about, and not wanting to have this conversation out in the open, Drew tried to dodge her questions. This seriousness was unusual for his baby sister. Drew had always worked so hard to shield her and protect her from as much ugliness as possible. But his bruised face was staring right back at her. Her worry for his safety made his chest twist.

Panda helped Drew to smile, trying to reassure his sister. But his words came out sounding fake. "It's fine. Don't worry about it."

Evie wasn't fooled by that answer. Or his phony mood. Her worried pout turned angry as Drew lied to her. "*Shit! Why is she so smart?*" Panda questioned as Drew's heart sank. "*She must be thinking it's Liam. But how could she know it IS Liam?*"

"Drew," Evie started to protest again.

"We'll talk about it later," Drew answered hurriedly. He patted her on the back reassuringly. Her face smoothed out once more. She leaned in and hugged her brother tightly. Drew wasn't sure if the hug was for her benefit or for his. But he wasn't about to turn down this affection from her. He picked her up and held her tightly as they all waited for Maddison. Muscle memory couldn't resist slightly bouncing her up and down. She felt like a baby again in his arms like this. Panda gently stroked her back.

Once Miranda's little sister joined them, he put Evie down so she and Maddy could walk together. This also gave Drew a moment to hold Miranda's hand a bit longer. He noticed his sister's social energy battery was severely depleted. "*She's worried about you, dumbass,*" Panda reflected.

As they walked up to Miranda's house, Evie turned abruptly to Drew and he nearly walked into her. "I wanna go home." Her voice had an icy tone to it that caused a chill to go up Drew's spine.

Drew hesitated as he attempted to find a good excuse to not go home. Evie's head tilted to the side as she looked up at him, squinting a bit from the sun. She was challenging the promise he made to her weeks ago, *"That we would take her home when she wanted"* Panda reminded Drew what he had said the first time he took Evie to Miranda's house.

"Are you sure, Evie?" Miranda bent down a bit, "My mom is going to order pizza. Last day of school tradition."

Evie stubbornly crossed her arms. Drew knew what her answer was. After squeezing Miranda's hand, he released it and Miranda nodded understandingly at him. Drew got on his bike. Evie waved goodbye and Drew bit back his disappointment as Miranda and Maddy waved back. He held his bike steady and Evie firmly planted her feet on the back tire pegs and gripped the sides of Drew's shirt for dear life. He knew how much she hated holding onto him like this. But it was the fastest way back without her bike. He pedaled to their house slowly and carefully.

"How was school, Eves?" he asked, turning his head slightly so she could hear him. He hoped her mood would brighten up the more she kept talking.

She shrugged against him. "It was good. Artemis's mom

brought cupcakes. And Mrs. Spencer let us have a movie day."

"What movie did you watch?" Panda asked from his skateboard.

"Finding Nemo." Drew could hear the smile in her voice. "Faith is having a sleepover this weekend. Can I go?"

Drew's head bobbed in recollection. "Isn't there another sleepover going on?"

"That's Charlotte. Tonight. You said I could go." She squeezed his abdomen tighter as he made a turn. He patted at her small hands in reassurance.

"That's if Mom's working. We'll have to double check."

"Ok," she sighed. "What about Faith?"

"What about her?" Drew gently weaved along the empty street.

"Can I go to her sleepover?"

"Eves, I don't know," Drew answered a little too sharply. Her grip tightened again, but not from Drew's steering. Drew released a regrettable sigh. "I'm sorry, Eves. We'll have to check with Mom."

"Is Mom home?" she asked quietly, unsure of what caused her brother's outburst.

"I don't know," Drew answered honestly.

They rounded the corner and Drew coasted for a bit on their street. *"What if Liam's home?"* Drew felt Panda's panic rise along with his own. His body grew rigid. His hands tightened on the handlebars. Evie noticed his tension.

"Drew?" Evie asked gently. "You ok?"

He forced air into his lungs, "Yeah, I'm ok."

"Think we can ask for pizza tonight? Like Maddy and Miranda?" she asked full of hope, her happy nature slowly returning.

Drew chuckled. "I think that's a great question for Mom."

As they came up to their house, Drew slightly relaxed. The garage door was still open. Celeste's car rested in the driveway and Liam's car was nowhere to be found. *"Thank God!"*

"Mom's home!" Evie pointed out when the car came into her view.

Drew waited for Evie to hop off his bike before he leaned it against the garage wall. He closed the massive rolling door and then dragged his feet in behind his sister.

"Mom!" Evie called out.

Celeste rushed into the hall from the dining room. Her eyes seemed too wide. Her cheeks more hollow than usual. She bent over and scooped Evie up into a tight hug. Evie didn't seem bothered and hugged her mom back just as tightly. But Drew was more wary. The last time he saw his mom this disheveled was last year when she told them that his dad had passed away.

Celeste looked over at Drew. The hand that rested on Evie's back twitched. She wanted to reach out to her son. She wanted to console him just as much.

Drew kept his hands in his pockets and leaned against the wall with judgmental observation.

"We need to talk," Celeste rushed out.

"Where's Liam?" Drew tried to bite back Panda's growl. Drew refused to drop his guard now that the secret was out.

"Not here." Celeste shook her head.

"Evie has a question." He jerked his chin to his little sister who looked like she might explode.

Celeste turned her head to look at her. Evie, still in her arms, erupted, "Charlotte is having a sleepover tonight. Drew said I could go. Can I? And Faith is having a sleepover this Friday. Drew said to ask you. Can I go?"

Celeste looked disoriented as her eyes settled on Drew. He stared at her with a heavy brow and crossed his arms, as if he were trying to psychically order his mom to give Evie the permission she craved. Their mom stammered for a moment before turning back to Evie, "Charlotte West and Faith Graham?" she asked as she flipped through her memory rolodex of Evie's classmates. When Evie nodded in confirmation, Celeste agreed, "Sure, sweetheart."

"To both?" Evie itemized.

Their mom gave her a pressed smile, her eyes weary. "Of course." Evie released a victorious cheer, causing a crack in Drew's hard exterior. His lips twitched in an attempt to smile and Celeste choked on a surprised chuckle. "I need to talk to your brother now. Why don't you go pack for tonight?" She gently returned her daughter to the ground.

Evie hurriedly ran off to her room. Drew felt better after seeing his sister's shift in mood. He knew he had bought himself some time before she asked him more questions about Liam and what happened to Drew's nose.

Celeste's smile dropped the moment Evie left the room.

She looked back at Drew before her eyes darted to the table. Clenching and unclenching her hands, she sat down. She eyed the chair in front of her, and then looked up at Drew, wordlessly telling him to sit down. Drew glanced down the hall and saw that Evie's door was half closed. Satisfied that she couldn't hear, he slowly sat down across from his mom.

"Where's Liam?" Panda repeated.

"I don't know," she grumbled. "And I don't care right now. He's never coming back here."

Drew's lips pressed into a tight line. His brow twitched in doubt. Panda released a heavy breath in relief.

"Drew," she reached her cold, surgical hands toward him. He pulled back, crossed his arms, and leaned back in his chair. His leg bounced up and down with edgy nerves. The movement caused Celeste to pause.

"Start from the beginning, Drew. What happened between you and your uncle?" Her face was stern, but her eyes were coated with tears.

"Why are you crying?" Drew asked harshly. "*It's not like she was the one who was abused!*" Panda noted bitterly. "*We're the ones who should be crying!*"

"Because I failed you, Drew. I need to know what happened." She shuddered. "When?"

Drew shook his head, looking down at a knot in the wood table. "It doesn't matter."

"Drew," his mom commanded sharply.

Her tone took him back. But he wasn't ready to give her sympathy. He looked at her with stone eyes. "Why does it matter if he's not coming back?" Drew snapped back.

Celeste licked at her lips. Her eyes fluttered as she tried to hold on to her tears. "Did he ever…with Evie?" she barely asked over a whisper.

Drew shook his head no. "I made sure of that," Panda growled in reply.

The tears she was working so hard to keep at bay flooded down her cheeks, like a dam gushing with water. She gasped for air and her voice squeaked, "Drew, I'm so sorry. Talk to me." Lowering her voice, she gained a bit more control. "What did he do? When did this happen?"

Drew sighed in response, running a frustrated hand through his dry scalp. "*Why does it even matter?*" Panda groaned.

"We're pressing charges!"

Drew's eyes snapped to her. Her tears stopped under his intense stare. He could see the sleek trail down her cheeks. "What are you talking about?"

Celeste shook her head as if the answer was obvious. "Liam can't get away with this…"

"He's gotten away with it now for four years!" Drew interrupted.

"You were thirteen?" Her eyes softened again.

"*Oh my God!*" Panda began pacing in quick, short,

frustrated steps in the living room. Drew sat up and loudly tapped the table with his index finger. "I'm not spending the whole summer in courtrooms, being humiliated, and re-living that whole moment again in a room full of strangers." Drew worked to keep his voice down, but he couldn't keep his anger out of it. "*Can't let Evie hear you,*" Panda warned.

Celeste sat up, matching Drew's anger. "But Drew…"

Drew slapped the table with his palm. The sudden impact made his mom flinch. "I said NO, Mom," Panda interrupted. "Just make sure Liam never comes back in this house again and that Evie NEVER comes in contact with him," Drew snarled through gritted teeth. "He's out?"

His mom nodded in earnest.

"Then he's out. For good."

Celeste nodded again, and then her head began to shake. Losing the direction of their conversation, she became a blubbering mess again. "Drew, I'm so sorry."

"Stop apologizing, Mom." Dismissing her sentiments, he leaned back, his face twisted in annoyance.

"Therapy then."

Panda choked on a laugh. "No," Drew answered. "I'm fine. And I will be fine if I never have to see Liam again."

"You're hurting yourself, honey," she wrung her hands in

uncertainty. "You clearly have anger issues."

Drew's body stiffened. "How dare you!" His eyes narrowed. "I only did it the one summer, when it happened. I haven't cut myself in four years." Drew said with finality, leaning against the table, his hands tucked against his chest. "*Well, you did let me cut you that one time last year when Dad died,*" Panda reminded Drew. It didn't matter, the sentiment was still the same. The thin layer of skin beneath Drew's knuckles whitened. "I've done nothing but help protect Evie better than you could've done."

Drew didn't care how harsh his words were. He could see the hurt in his mother's eyes. At the same time, her eyes locked on his and her face hardened, as if a switch went off inside her. "You don't have a choice in this. You are my son. I will not allow this to be swept under the rug. It's either a courtroom full of strangers or one room with one stranger."

"Or else…" Drew pushed, trying to call her bluff.

"I'll press charges for you," she threatened. "You're still a minor, Drew. And Liam's crime has not exceeded the statute of limitation."

His nose flared. His hands began to ache under their strain. "You can't be serious."

"I'm very serious, Drew." The calmness in Celeste's

voice caused chills to run up Drew's spine. Her face softened again as she blinked a few times. "You choose. But I expect a decision by tomorrow."

"Tomorrow?!" Drew shrieked.

His mom nodded. "We're not letting this fester any longer." She released a heavy sigh before being overcome with exhaustion. She shook her head and mumbled, "It all makes sense now."

Drew watched as his mom put the dots together. Why he quit football. Why his behavior changed. His change in clothing. His grades plummeting that last semester of eighth grade. Why Drew had been so angry since Liam moved in. His crusade to always babysit Evie. It all clicked. And she hated herself for missing all the clues Drew had given her.

Panda barked out a laugh, interrupting Drew's study of his mom. *"If she wanted to help, then she should've paid more attention that spring break! She should've paid more attention to us! She shouldn't have disappeared after Dad died! We NEEDED her!"*

Drew leaned back like his mom. Exhaustion had started to settle in his bones too. He weighed his options as Panda continued to lay blame on his mom. Drew could feel Panda's anger at being abused, abandoned, and cornered by his mom just below his skin. He wanted to claw it out. But Drew could also feel the vast sorrow of it all. He was so tired of trying to bury everything.

Drew couldn't see a way out. His mom had failed him. Sure. Panda wasn't wrong about that. But Drew had failed himself too. He could've said something to his parents all those years ago. He could have said something when Liam suggested he move in. Maybe done more to help his mom. But he was too lost in his own grief and pain to see that his mom was in pain too. That she needed him just as badly as he needed her. He was too angry to see what Celeste and Liam were doing under his own nose, too withdrawn into his own problems to really help his family the way he wanted to help. The way they truly needed him.

"I'll think about it," Drew finally conceded. Sincerity and fear of the unknown tickled the back of his throat.

CHAPTER EIGHTEEN

"*Oh, mah gawd!*" Panda dragged his hands down his furry face in exaggeration. "*Today has been the longest day in existence!*" he shouted from his skateboard as Drew determinedly biked across town.

"Yeah," Drew agreed, his head high. "And it's not over yet!" He felt reinvigorated with purpose.

Panda whined in protest. "*Can't we wait to see Omar tomorrow?*"

Drew stiffly shook his head. His mouth turned down. "No. We're getting this done. No more. I'm out. Liam's out. We're getting a new start." Omar had texted twenty minutes ago that Drew could come by. He was not going to waste this opportunity.

"*Can you believe the nerve of Celeste?*"

Drew could practically taste the disgust that dripped from Panda's mouth. He shrugged in indifference. He didn't feel like arguing the point right now. "Just be lucky she didn't threaten to lock us up in the psych ward at the hospital."

"*Shit*," Panda thought about it. "*Good point. Are we really going to a therapist?*"

Drew didn't want to do a deep psychological dive of how he was to blame for so many things, too. Instead, he tried to block the whole ordeal. He had to focus right now.

They stopped at the lamppost on the corner of the apartment building, and Drew locked his bike while Panda hid his skateboard nearby. Drew glanced around the neighborhood for a minute. "*Dude, we might need a quick exit just in case things don't go as planned,*" Panda warned. Drew turned the numbers to his code. One tug and the chain would be undone. "I hope nobody messes with my bike while we're gone!"

Drew picked his head up and was startled to see an older man sitting outside on a rickety foldout chair that had seen better days. Drew clamped his mouth shut, not wanting anyone to see him talking to himself. The man's experienced eyes slowly dragged over everything, taking in the kids playing on the community picnic table like a jungle gym, the few joggers passing by, and the dog pressed up against the gate across the street barking at anyone who came within a five-foot radius of it. Those old, faded eyes took in Drew, too, and studied him carefully. Biting back his response to Panda, Drew said a quick hello to the man as he walked by, getting a respectable nod in return. Panda awkwardly waved to him as he tiptoed behind Drew. Drew and Panda could feel the old man's eyes burning into their backs.

"*Drew?*" Panda whispered when he was sure they were out of ear shot.

"What?" Drew hissed.

"*You never answered my question.*"

"About?" Drew rolled his eyes.

"*Are we going to a therapist?*"

Drew's face twitched with uncertainty. "What? I don't know. You heard Mom." Drew shook his head, thinking about the ultimatum he was given. Pressing charges against his uncle or therapy. And even though he'd rather do any-thing besides go see a therapist, it was probably very likely he would be seeing one.

"*Really?*" Panda questioned, hearing Drew's thoughts. "*Think we'll really never see Liam again?*"

"We better not!" Drew growled as he knocked on the door. He worked to relax his face as they waited.

The door creaked open. Omar hesitantly opened the door. "Drew…oh, shit!" he chuckled to himself when he took in the state of Drew's face. "Bro, what the fuck happened to your face?"

Drew forced a smile, "You should see the other guy."

Omar barked out a laugh, "Alright, if that's what's up, that's what's up." He hurried Drew inside. "Get in here, man." Omar looked both ways outside before closing the door and locking it twice with the deadbolt and then the chain lock.

Last time, the air reeked of weed and old socks. Now, it just smelled like old socks. The blinds and windows were open, letting in as much natural light and air as possible without using electricity. The dirty carpet was considerably more noticeable under the honest light. A cartoon blared on the TV. Jay laughed throatily on the couch as he watched the screen. The plump little boy Drew saw last time sat beside Jay. He clutched at his pudgy toes in comfort. A scrawny little girl, "*maybe no older than Evie*," Panda noticed, was cuddled against the massive man. Her knobby knees swayed slightly with each ripple from Jay's gut. She had her fingers in her mouth, biting her nails, and her frizzy hair looked like it hadn't been washed in days.

The woman with long pink braids sat crisscrossed on the floor in front of the coffee table, working. The low, rectangular wood table was packed with two sets of scales, a money counter, a whole pile of small plastic bags, and freezer bags stuffed with various pills and weed. Using her talon nails, she plucked prescription pills from a pile and placed them in small baggies. She didn't look up from her task as Drew came in.

"I've got the rest of the money," Drew hesitated as he got a good look around.

"Oh shit," Omar turned to him. "See, you be hustlin' better than the other wanna be lil' gangsters I've got comin' and goin'." He snapped his fingers at Drew, demanding his backpack. Drew hurriedly handed over his bag. "Nat!" he snapped at the woman. "Pass the counter," he said dropping down in a chair.

Popping her gum and rolling her eyes, she handed him the machine. He set it down and fed Drew's money into it. The machine whirred as it counted the bills. The kids didn't seem bothered as the sound of the machine drowned out some of their show. Drew and Panda stood quietly to the side, blocking the sun for Omar.

The machine finally silenced. "Looks good, man. There's even more here. What'd you do?"

Drew released the breath he didn't realize he was holding. "I charged a bit more this time…you know… parting on good terms and all."

Omar hummed in thought, appreciating Drew's way of business.

"Listen," Drew continued, "I'll head out then. Thanks for everything, Omar." He headed for the door and only managed to unlock the deadbolt.

"You just got here, man. Why don't you hang a bit?" Omar gestured to the empty chair, the one Nat was sitting in the last time he was there.

Drew took a half a step back. "Oh, I can't. I've got somewhere to be."

"Like where?" Omar's tone turned sharp. His yellow eyes watched Drew like a hawk.

Drew timidly waved his thumb at the door. As if the motion would magically open it and thrust him out of the apartment. "I've got a thing with my friend."

Omar snapped his fingers at him in remembrance. "Your party. That tonight?"

Drew cleared his throat. "Yeah," Panda blurted out, panicking, not able to lie.

"Oh, good!" Omar turned back around and snapped repeatedly at Nat.

She groaned, "Stop snappin' at me. Can't you see I'm busy?!" She continued her task.

"Fuckin' bitch," Omar growled beneath his breath. "You better fix your attitude, woman!" He grabbed a wad of loaded freezer bags and started piling them into Drew's backpack himself.

"Omar…" Drew said hesitantly. Panda's eyes widened in panic.

"You got mad cash flow for me, Drew." He held out the backpack for Drew to take.

Drew stared at the very thing that literally weighed down his back. It was an enabler to his peers, a burden to his mom, and made Evie bear witness to the ugliness of the world. His greatest regret. "Omar…I thought we were good."

"After this party," Omar shook Drew's backpack at him.

Drew flinched. "And then after the party?"

He sighed tiredly, "Then you're done."

"*He's lying,*" Panda advised. "*What if he keeps pushing you for the whole summer?! What if we get caught? We can't get put away!*" Drew shook his head and he and Panda took a nervous step backward toward the door. The movement caught Nat's and Jay's attention. Animated cartoon voices from the TV filled the room, swirling around the building tension.

Drew held his hands up in defense as he quickly tried to work out a plan with Panda to make a run for it. "Omar, my man, I can't. I won't work for anyone else, either. I promise."

Before Omar could say anything, Drew jumped as the door behind him slammed open.

He and Panda turned, taking several steps back into the small apartment as three men pushed themselves through the broken door. Drew's heart hitched into his throat. The kids on the couch screamed and cried at the sudden invasion. Jay tried to push them behind him, acting as a human shield. Nat's gum popping silenced as her hands paused midair above the coffee table.

Omar sprang to his feet. "The fuck you think you doin', Wallace, bouncin' in like this?"

"Shut them kids up!" Wallace ordered.

He was light skinned like Drew. His bald head shone in the light. He was taller than Omar by a foot and was just as big as Jay. But Jay used his fat to hurl his attacks. Wallace was all muscle. *"How else would you spend five years in prison?"* Panda wondered. Wallace was flanked on both sides by two of his men. They were both tall, but appeared considerably shorter and lankier next to Wallace. They both looked mean, ready to start a fight.

Without breaking eye contact, Omar yelled at Nat, "Get them out of here!"

Nat quickly stood and scooped up the screaming little boy and yanked on the little girl's arm nearly hurling her from the couch. She brushed past Drew, crossed in front of the two dueling drug dealers, and stormed down the hallway. The bedroom door slammed closed, barely muffling the children's crying. Jay stood up and moved beside Omar.

Drew watched the exchange from the sidelines, like an awkward third wheel he hoped no one would notice. He eyed the front door. He couldn't get out without shoving Wallace's thugs out the way.

Omar flung both arms out in a challenge. "The fuck you want?"

"We've got a problem, Omar," Wallace said in an authoritative tone. "My people tell me you're pushin' into my territory."

Drew's heart seized. His body became rigid. Drew HAD

encroached on Wallace's sector. He had been desperate to get rid of his shit quickly, but he'd only been on Wallace's turf for a few days. An hour here, an hour there. He didn't think the run-in he had last week would trace him back to Omar or that the guy had recognized him! "*Oh shit*," Panda breathed.

"No, I ain't!" Omar shot back.

"Then explain why this knuckle head has been sellin' on my streets." Wallace pointed at Drew. "My people saw his lanky ass last week. And we followed him to you."

Omar blinked at Drew. "What did you do?"

Drew threw up his hands. "Look, Wallace, my bad, man. Omar made me do it. I'm just trying to get out of this shit. I don't wanna sell anymore."

Omar's eyes flashed with anger. "Why you lyin'? I never told your dumb ass to sell over there!" Omar moved a step toward Drew like he was about to hit him.

In a blink of an eye, at Omar's movement, the man closest to Drew pulled a gun out from the front of his pants and pointed it at Omar. In response, Jay pulled a gun from the back of his pants and pointed it at Wallace. Then the other thug, Wallace, and Omar quickly pulled out guns and pointed them at each other. "*These things should only happen in old, Hollywood Westerns. Not real life!*" Panda assessed briskly.

Drew put his hands up on instinct in surrender and sheer panic, because everyone had a freaking gun except him, and in the wildest of hopes that if bullets went flying, his imaginary force shield would stop the assault.

Everyone started shouting at once.

"The fuck you thinkin', Wallace?"

"Shut the fuck up!"

"Put it down!"

"Fuck you!"

"You put it down!"

"Fuckin' bitch!"

Drew's heart raced a mile a second. He'd seen guns before, sure. He'd never been in a gun fight though! And he didn't want to start now. Wallace slowly extended his arms out to the side. Drew noticed his grip was still tight on the gun. But he'd moved it away from Omar's chest. At this, his two thugs stopped yelling, but they didn't lower their guns. Jay and Omar had quieted too.

"I want the money you took from me,." Wallace stated coolly.

"You take it off him," Omar pointed to Drew. "I didn't tell the fuckin' idiot to sell on your streets."

"You're in charge of him," Wallace shook his head, "I want it from you, punk bitch." He shoved a thick finger into Omar's thin chest.

Without thinking about it, Drew let Panda's adrenaline run his mouth, "Listen Wallace, Omar's got all my money. I don't have anything else on me." At this, he turned his front pockets inside out.

For the first time since he barged in, Wallace looked at Drew.

Drew's stomach dropped under Wallace's dark, analyzing eyes, but that didn't stop Panda's rambling. "I just want out. I'm not going to sell anymore. This was my last time with Omar. I've got my family to think about, man. My mom is working too much. I take care of my sister all the time. And without my dad, my mom needs extra help. I don't want to get in trouble again, Wallace…"

"How do you turn the Energizer Bunny off?" Wallace asked Omar harshly.

"Drew," Omar snapped at him, "shut the fuck up!"

Drew inhaled sharply. His heart hammered. His mouth was dry. His eyes darted back to the door. The escape he so desperately needed was still blocked by one of the thugs.

"Omar," Wallace's tone was ice, "give me my money you

stole, and we'll be on our way."

Omar took another step toward Wallace. One more step and their chests would touch. "Fuck you. And get the fuck outta my house."

Wallace chuckled and tucked his gun into his pants. Drew didn't understand the humor in any of this. His sides were beginning to cramp from the tension. Then Wallace punched Omar in the face. Jay and the other two thugs hesitantly kept their guns pointed at each other as their leaders swapped punches. Drew flinched as Wallace threw his whole weight into an uppercut to Omar's stomach. The man easily had another fifty pounds on scrawny Omar. Blood oozed from Omar's mouth.

On instinct, Drew crouched down behind the couch, fearful that bullets would soar through the air at any second. Jay and the others shouted incoherently at each other. The air filled with curses and grunting, drowning out everything. Drew's heart pounded in his ears. He heaved for air. His limbs buzzed. "*Drew, look!*" Panda pointed to the unguarded, open door.

In one swift motion, without thinking, Drew leapt up and sprinted through the door. His hip slammed into the outside railing. Straightening, he pumped his legs and ran toward the stairwell, skipping two, three steps at a time until he reached the bottom of the apartment building. The old man on his lawn chair was gone. So were the kids playing outside. Panting, he yanked his bike chain off the lamppost and threw the lock on the ground. He hurled himself on his bike and furiously pedaled away.

Drew made it down the street and skidded around the corner when he heard a lone gunshot echo through the neighborhood. Gasping, Drew kept biking. His shirt was soaked in sweat, his legs burned, and his lungs begged him to stop. He kept pedaling as fast as he could while Panda scrambled to keep up on his skateboard.

CHAPTER NINETEEN

"*Holy shit,*" Panda gasped.

Drew had never pedaled so hard in his life. The echo of the gun going off roared in his ears. He gasped, desperate for air. He blinked wildly, his cautious eyes darting all around him.

"*Holy shit!*" Panda repeated. He was in just as much shock as Drew. "*I can't believe that happened!*"

"Do you think Omar will be after us?" Drew's voice was raspy and he was dying for some water.

"*He knows where we live, right?*"

"What do we do now?"

"*Does this mean we're done?*"

Drew sighed heavily. He forced himself to take in air. "I think we're done so long as we stay away from them."

The two silently headed to Trey's. Every decision Drew made that had led him to Omar, and his life as a drug dealer, was forefront in his mind. Panda occasionally interrupted, recounting every moment of their encounter with Wallace and the crippling fear when they saw everyone pull their guns out, and panicking that Wallace would turn on him like Omar had.

Drew could have died.

He would've died in that filthy apartment. Drew thought about how they probably would have just dumped his body at the hospital. Maybe the same hospital his mom worked at. Is that how his mom would've seen him? A crumpled up heap carelessly dropped off outside the ER? Lifeless. And the last conversation he had with his mom was over his abusive uncle. He had said spiteful things to her. Would she remember him by their last conversation? And Evie. She'd grow up without him. And Wynter and Trey. How much would they mourn him before they moved on with their lives?

"*Dude!*" Panda interrupted Drew's train of thought. "*None of that matters! We're alive!*"

Drew nearly choked with relief as he absorbed what Panda said. He exhaled deeply and his breathing began to regulate once again. His sweaty, damp shirt caused a cold chill as he biked. Drew couldn't contain his widespread grin as Panda howled loudly, rejoicing in their newfound freedom.

"We're celebrating tonight, right?"

"Absolutely!" Drew affirmed. It had been one hell of a day.

"How shall we celebrate?" Panda heckled sarcastically.

"Weed and alcohol sounds like a good start to me."

"Nope!" Panda violently shook his head. *"Remember what happened at Devón's party last year?"* He didn't wait for a response from Drew. *"You decided to mix the two, blacked out, freaked out Wynter, threw up everywhere, and then crashed on Trey's floor. Embarrassing! I'm not going through that again."*

Drew cringed at Panda's stroll down memory lane. "You're the one who had the terrible idea to mix Sprite and Vodka that night."

Panda pursed his lips. *"Touché. Let's just get high tonight. It's been a while and a lot better than risking alcohol poisoning."*

Drew suppressed a chuckle. "Sounds like a plan."

"Hey," Panda swerved in front of Drew on his skateboard, cutting him off with growing excitement. *"Do you think Miranda is coming?"*

Drew came to a screeching halt at a stop sign. "Knock it

off," Drew warned in growing annoyance.

Panda disregarded Drew's irritation. *"Text her!"* With shaky balance, Drew pulled out his phone. But he paused. His heart cramped he saw a text from his mom.

CELESTE: Hey. I'm checking in. You doing ok?

Drew pressed his mouth into a thin line, worried that if he didn't, it would tremble. For the first time in years, Drew craved a hug from his mom. He wanted to feel the safety that only a parent can provide with their tight embrace. Sniffing hard, he cleared his vision, then texted his mom.

DREW: I'm good. I'm hanging out with Trey and Wynter tonight. I'll be back home later.

CELESTE: Thanks for letting me know. I'm getting ready to take Evie to her sleepover. I'm on call tonight. But let me know if you need anything!

DREW: thanks mom

Drew sighed deeply. He felt his adrenaline starting to ease piece by piece. Then he texted Miranda at the behest of Panda.

DREW: Are you coming to Trey's tonight?

MIRANDA: Depends…are you going?

DREW: yes

MIRANDA: Then I'll be there 😊

DREW: can't wait

"*She is soooooooo in love with us!*" Panda squealed like a little girl.

"Take a chill pill," Drew bit his bottom lip. Love was a big word. He liked Miranda, of course. And cared about her. Was this what love feels like? He thought it'd be grander and more romantic like those movies Celeste was obsessed with.

MIRANDA: I'm coming with Sydney. Would that be weird?

DREW: We'll keep them separated…

Drew put his phone back in his pocket and biked swiftly to Trey's. He opened the back gate and wedged his bike in the backyard, making a mental note to buy a new lock. Satisfied his bike was safe, he and Panda walked into Trey's house with vigor in their step. Trey was at the kitchen island with Wynter. She sat on the counter, watching him open the fifth bag of chips.

"Sup," Drew announced as he made a beeline toward the cups.

Their collective "hey" was muffled as Drew hurriedly grabbed a cup, filled it up with tap water, and greedily downed it. Small trickles of water spilled out the corners of his mouth. Filling it up again, he gulped a second cup down.

He wiped his chin and turned around to find his best friends staring at him as he panted heavily.

He cleared his throat and set the cup by the sink. He hungrily helped himself to a handful of chips, the violent rumble in his stomach too loud to ignore.

"Dude," Wynter hopped off the counter.

"What?" Drew shoved a chip in his mouth.

His friends' eyes were wide, taking in his appearance. Drew had sweat patches all over his red shirt from running away from Omar's. His face was bruised from his earlier fight with Liam. He suddenly realized that he looked like a hot mess. Wynter came closer to him. The slight brush of her fingers against his cheek caused butterflies in his stomach. Unable to handle his growing nerves feeling her touch him, he swerved his head away from her. With a scowl, she backed up. Leaning against the kitchen island, she waited for Drew to explain further.

"What happened to you?" Trey questioned.

"Oh…" Drew shook his head. "*Where to begin?*" Panda stood back and peered at Drew's face, wondering if his nose still looked bad. "…I got into it with Liam."

"What?!" Wynter gasped. Panda and Drew cringed at her shrill voice. "What happened?"

Drew shrugged as he thought about telling them. He mulled it over with another chip. "I found out he and my mom were fucking," Drew answered with revulsion, picking up another chip, "and then I punched him in the face. Then he punched me. And my mom kicked him out." Wynter and Trey looked at each other with grave faces.

"Is that why you're so sweaty?" Wynter asked. It wasn't that hot outside for him to sweat through his clothes.

"Uh…" Drew looked down at his shirt. "I just left Omar's." He looked at both of them. "Dude…" Panda was eager to tell them everything but Drew decided against it. He'd tell Trey everything that happened later. He didn't want to worry Wynter right now. "I'm out!" he finally declared, smiled proudly.

"Out out?" Trey squinted at him.

"Out out." Drew confirmed with pride. With a triumphant grin, Trey moved closer and grabbed Drew in a hug. He slapped his back like a proud dad. When they pulled away, Wynter blinked at him in bewilderment. She seemed frozen in place. "What?" Drew said as he shoved another handful of chips in his mouth. "*When was the last time we ate?*" Panda mused. He couldn't remember.

"You ok?" Her question was soft. She wasn't sure where

to start unpacking Drew's dramatic day.

Trey shrugged. "We know you didn't really like your uncle…"

Drew was never completely honest with his best friends about what Liam did to him. Shame made him barricade himself against possible judgment. They figured out on their own that Liam was abusive in some way from the way Drew talked about him and from their own observations when they came over. They could never guess just how abusive. They knew Drew would tell them when he was ready, so they never interrogated him for more information. Looking at his best friends, Drew felt guilty for keeping such a big secret from them. But he cherished them immensely for their support.

"*You might as well tell them the whole truth now,*" Panda urged. "*Mom finally knows what happened. So, tell them! What more harm could it do? Just get it over with. Rip off the Band-Aid!*"

Drew didn't have the energy to entertain Panda's pushing. Today had already been traumatic for him phy-sically, and emotionally with Liam and his mom earlier. Then psychologically with and his near-death traumatic experience in Omar's apartment. Drew did not want to add more to this day by revealing the abuse he'd survived to his friends. He knew they'd be supportive and understanding. But Drew decided he would tell them when he had the emotional bandwidth. Not now, when he was so mentally exhausted.

"You know," Drew thought about it for a moment, "I haven't felt this ok since before my dad died."

Trey gave him a tight-lipped smile. Wynter, biting back her concern, walked around the kitchen island to hug him. Drew waved Trey over. The three embraced in a giant hug. After a few solitary seconds, Trey squeezed them. Wynter laughed as she was squished in the middle.

That joyful laugh was enough to break the tension. It was now summer vacation! Trey let Drew borrow one of his black shirts after Drew cleaned himself up. The three of them took first dibs on the snacks and got the fire pit going in the back yard. Trey's parents were gone for the weekend, maintaining the tradition of giving their son run of the house on the last day of school. They trusted him to have a few friends over to welcome summer, not really knowing their son's level of popularity. Trey was just fortunate he had two best friends to help him clean up after the whole class showed up at his house.

By the time the sun disappeared around eight o'clock, the

music started up, the lights turned down low, and people started rolling through. It took Drew at least an hour to explain to people that he didn't have anything to sell. Fortunate for them, someone else was able to supply. *"One less thing to worry about! Can we party now?"* Panda pleaded.

Drew, Wynter, and Trey claimed three lawn chairs in the back yard around the fire pit and passed around a bowl of freshly packed weed. Panda eagerly took it for his turn. He hated the bowl. He much preferred a pen. But beggars can't be choosers. Lighting a small corner of the fresh weed, he released his thumb and inhaled. As always, he burned his thumb. He never noticed the dull pain until after he passed the material on to the next person. Panda held his breath. He always seemed to forget how to swallow at this part. His eyes burned as he forced the substance down his throat. Calmly, he unevenly breathed out his nose and then inhaled sharply. Finally managing to swallow, Panda forced the smoke down into Drew's lungs. Exhaling steadily, he held onto his cough. Panda really didn't smoke enough to feel confident he was doing it correctly.

As the THC traveled to their brain, Drew and Panda sat back. Drew's eyes were instantly heavy. Panda began to float, swimming in circles around him, content. Relaxed even. It'd been a minute since Drew smoked. "*Since last year*," Panda reminded. Drew took one more hit once the bowl made it back to him. The small bowl looked like a half-scorched green lawn. He skipped his turn as the bowl made its next lap. Slow burning embers rested in his chest. His throat was sore and his nose runny. Drew dropped his head back and stared up at the sky.

"It's so beautiful," Panda slipped out.

"What is?" Wynter responded as she focused on repacking the bowl.

"The sky is just so pretty," Panda clarified. Drew lazily turned his head. Wynter's hooded grey eyes looked at him. "But your eyes are even better," Panda said.

"*Shit!*" Drew gawked to himself. This was why he didn't smoke! It was too challenging to contain Panda. The weed stripped away Drew's ability to keep Panda's thoughts quiet.

Wynter blushed and looked away. "*You need to keep your mouth shut!*" Drew protested, but Panda ignored him. He was too preoccupied with watching his best friend in slow motion. Panda looked around. He was getting more comfortable as he took control of Drew's body. "Wyn is so beautiful," Panda quietly remarked. "And like, our best friend. Why aren't we with HER?"

Drew argued back, "*Because she IS our best friend! She doesn't even like us like that.*"

Panda didn't retort. Drew's chest ached.

CHAPTER TWENTY

Panda picked his head up and looked around the smoke circle. A slow smile spread across his lips, welcoming his friends' inner monsters that began taking shape the more everyone got high. They were enjoying the weed as much as their host body. A giant grizzly bear had taken over Trey's body. Panda looked back to Wynter. In her place was the most beautiful, humanoid, raccoon girl he had ever seen. And she winked at him. Butterflies erupted at the gesture. "*NO!*" Drew managed to get back behind the wheel for a second, suddenly thrusting himself onto his feet.

"You good?" the raccoon girl asked, furrowing her dark brows.

"Yeah," Drew huffed, "I'm just going to head inside for a minute." Drew dragged himself and Panda back into the house. "*Oh chips!*" Panda navigated their body to the kitchen. Drew didn't know how long they stood there, but at least Panda's mouth was occupied by food. Drew's phone buzzed in his pocket. With salt-coated fingers, he pulled his phone out. It was a text from Miranda.

MIRANDA: We're here! Where are you?

DREW: kitchen

Panda scanned the crowd for her. Drew's stomach knotted. He was excited to see Miranda, but he could feel his control of Panda slipping. He didn't trust Panda not to say anything stupid. They saw her before she spotted them, like a bright beacon parting the crowd. She had her hair down in large brown waves. Her white tank top was tucked into a pair of denim shorts. Panda wondered if Sydney dressed her for the occasion. Miranda slowly turned her head round, looking for him.

When Miranda's bright eyes met his, she smiled widely and gently made her way to him.

"Miranda!" Panda hugged her excitedly, swaying side to side. "*Ah! Dude! Get your salty fingers off of her!*" Drew panicked. She giggled into his chest.

She pulled her face back to look at Drew. Her smile faltered a bit. "Glad to see you in a good mood."

"I'm fantastic!" Panda yelled when he didn't need to since he was standing so close to her.

"Are you high?" She tried to keep her voice calm, but her posture was ramrod straight.

Panda snorted, "Only a little bit."

Her forehead creased slightly. She was caught off-guard seeing Drew like this. "Are you sure that's a good idea?"

Panda nodded his head emphatically. "It's a great idea! I'm done with Omar! I'm done with Liam! My mom knows everything now! I'm great!"

She stared at him. The name Omar didn't sound familiar to her. Miranda had many more questions for him. Mainly if getting high was the smartest idea for Drew and if this was a habit she should expect. But what Sydney told her as they approached the party niggled the back of her mind, "Don't be a buzz kill." So, instead of asking more questions like she wanted, she said, "Where's Trey?"

"Back yard," Panda answered a little too loudly. Suddenly self-conscious of his possible nacho chip breath, he washed his mouth out with some soda. "Why?"

Miranda looked around. "Sydney's around here some-where." They had become separated when Miranda found Drew.

Suppressing a sudden oncoming burp from the carbonated soda, Panda waved her off and said, "I'm sure they'll be fine." He knew Trey would avoid Sydney at all costs. Trey's heart was still fragile from their breakup.

Miranda looked back at him. She didn't agree at all. She knew that Sydney would probably pick a fight with Trey on purpose.

Panda took a step back, soaking her in. "You're pretty," he blurted out. "*Would you shut up!*" Drew cringed. "*We can't just go around telling every girl she's pretty.*"

With flushed cheeks, she leaned in closer, "Come dance with me."

Panda practically slammed his soda down on the counter. Small droplets landed on his hand as he followed her without hesitation to the living room, the source of the loud music. They danced. But not at all like they did at prom. Miranda was closer. MUCH CLOSER. Her back pressed into his chest. Panda kept her in place with his hands on her rotating hips. Her soft, wavy brown locks brushed against his furry face and he inhaled her intoxicating strawberry scent.

The crowd increased, pushing the two of them closer against the wall. Drew was fine with that. He figured Panda could do minimal damage by dancing quietly in the corner of the room. Miranda turned around and, pressing herself into him more. Her arms caged him in at the neck. "*This is nice,*" Drew thought to nag Panda for once. "*See, you idiot, we have Miranda. Let's ask her to be our girlfriend! Or should we do that when we're sober? For sure wait until we're sober.*"

Miranda leaned closer to Panda's mouth, pressing into him for leverage as she reached for his lips on her toes. Drew braced himself for their kiss. "Did you spread that rumor about Wynter?" Panda blurted out before it even passed the filtered-thoughts test. Drew felt like cold water had been thrown on him. He couldn't believe Panda had just said that.

"What?" Miranda blinked back at him.

"Wynter," Panda continued, "she told me you and Porter started that whole 'Quick Winter' rumor thing." She dropped back down to her heels and took a step back from him. Her dark brows were bunched in the middle.

Shocked by this turn of events, Miranda put a hand on his arm. "Drew," she tried to steer him out of the living room. "Why don't we go somewhere else to talk."

Panda ignored her suggestion and shrugged her hand off him. "Did you have anything to do with that?" Panda interrogated. Drew watched the confrontation in shock. He felt embarrassed that Panda had started this. But he wanted to know what she'd say.

Miranda shook her head furiously. "That was all Sydney. I…"

"Did you try to stop it?"

"Of course," she hugged herself. "I didn't spread those rumors. I didn't even say anything."

"You didn't say ANYTHING?" Panda's eyes squinted, confused. She shook her head in confirmation. "Did you ever think that by not saying anything, it was just as hurtful?"

"Sydney was the one dragging her name through the mud." Miranda took another step back. Her voice competed with the music.

"But you didn't stand up for Wynter! And you stayed friends with a bully!" Panda shouted back. A few heads turned. Miranda stood and stared at him. Her nose flared as she tried to keep her emotions in check. But her eyes were huge and round, as if she was trying to keep herself from crying.

"Why are you acting like this?"

He barely heard her over the music. That question splintered his heart. Panda blinked at her a few times. His anger for his friend ebbed as it saw the hurt on Miranda's face. "*What are we doing?*" Drew echoed. "I have to go," Panda hushed out. He turned and pushed against the nosy crowd.

Panda returned to the stoner circle he had left what felt like years ago. He sat down between the beautiful raccoon and the hulking grizzly bear.

"Dude," Trey's bear pushed against his shoulder, "where'd you go?"

"I got some chips," Panda mumbled.

"What's up with you?" the bear squinted at him.

Panda shook his head in dismissal. He inhaled deeply from the bowl when it made its way to him. After burning his thumb again from the lighter, he passed the weed on to Wynter's raccoon. She watched him warily. Her large steely eyes were a pool of empathy.

"You ok?" she placed a warm hand on his arm.

He stared down at her hand. It was the source of so much warmth. "I'm fine," Panda shrugged.

To his disappointment, Wynter removed her hand, but her concerned look didn't disappear. "*Actually,*" Panda sighed tiredly, "*I'm done driving.*" Panda gave Drew back the controls.

Drew was drained. He slumped down in the lawn chair.

"Hey Trey!" Drew turned his head when he heard his friend's name. Drew didn't recognize the guy who was crouched down with his hand on Trey's shoulder. "You've got to come inside, man. Sydney is throwing a fit."

"Oh shit," Trey sluggishly stood up to follow the guy into the house.

The backyard cleared as everyone swarmed into the house to watch the impending drama. Wynter's face twisted with uncertainty. She wasn't sure which friend she should support. Drew seemed to have a thousand-yard stare about him, the flicking flames of the fire pit consuming his attention.

"I'll be right back." Wynter patted his arm, got up, and left him. Drew immediately missed the warmth her brief touch gave him.

After she left, Drew cursed at Panda, "Why did you have to say all that shit to Miranda?"

"I don't know! I couldn't help it. We were so close to having a girlfriend too! I just kept thinking of Wynter. Trey was brave enough to stand up to Sydney. Wyn is our best friend. We should've done the same! We knew Wynter was bullied. But classic Drew, you ignored your best friend's feelings and went after Miranda anyways just because she was nice to us. You didn't want to lose that. Well guess what! I wasn't going to let us lose Wynter either! Why don't you get off your pathetic ass and go be with your other best friend as

he wars against his ex?" Panda berated.

"I can't do any damage by sitting here, now can I?" Drew grumbled.

Drew turned his head slightly toward the lit-up house. He heard jeers and yelling from where he sat. Panda continued to poke at him, urging him to get up. Eventually, Drew wanted to, but he couldn't seem to get his limbs to work. After a few minutes, the noise seemed to settle and the music came back on, much louder this time. People slowly dispersed from the center of the house and leaked into the backyard, coming outside to mingle. A few even rejoined the circle.

Trey stomped toward them, his bear gone. The fight must have sobered him up. Drew craned his neck. Wynter wasn't behind him. Trey sighed loudly as he sat down in his chair beside Drew.

"What happened?" Drew asked groggily.

Trey groaned, running a hand down his face. "What happened between you and Miranda?"

Drew shrugged, not wanting to talk about it. "What's that got to do with anything?"

"Well…" Trey bent his head side to side. Bones cracked with each movement. "According to Sydney, you yelled at her for no reason. She said that you are a fucked up, drug dealer who uses people."

Drew flinched at Sydney's words. "*Is she right?*" Panda mused.

"Now," Trey sighed, his tone softening a bit, "I ask again. What happened between you and Miranda?"

"What'd you say to Sydney?"

Trey shrugged. "I told her she had no right talking shit about my friends. That I was tired of her being a bully. And then I kicked her out."

Drew snapped his head up to his friend. "Did Miranda go with?" Trey nodded his head yes. Drew slumped in his chair again. "*Trey is a better friend than you are,*" Panda criticized. "*He stands up for the people he cares about.*" Eventually Drew answered, "I asked Miranda about Wynter."

"And?" Trey leaned back and laced his fingers together on his lap.

Drew shook his head. "I blew up at her because she didn't stop Sydney from spreading those rumors."

Trey waited a few moments. "Well…now you know."

Drew didn't answer.

"So why are you being like this now?" He waved a hand over Drew's mopey body.

Drew turned his head slightly toward Trey, "What do you mean?"

"This is a party, dude. My party. I know you had a rough day, man, but Jesus. Lighten up. So you got into an argument with Miranda. It's not the end of the world."

"But it is the end of the world!" Panda ranted. *"We lost our one chance to get a girlfriend. We couldn't stand up for our best friend. And our other best friend just got into it with his ex because of us. We don't know what's waiting for us at home. We're probably going to see a therapist. I'd rather die than go to court. And who knows if Omar is going to just let us go or not after we ran away!"*

Drew inhaled sharply. "Trey…" His chest ached to unload everything on him.

Trey sat up when he saw the look on his friend's face, like the entire world was on his shoulders. "Look dude, I know things have been rough lately," Trey's tone was gentle. "But I'm not going to lie. You have a habit to self-destruct. Especially when things go good." He put a big, meaty hand on Drew's shoulder. "But you've got to give yourself some grace. You deserve to be happy, Drew. Just like everyone else. Just like everyone you try to take care of."

Drew's eyes started to water.

"You deserve to be happy," Trey repeated quietly.

Drew leaned forward and dug the heel of his palms into his eyes, resisting the urge to cry. Panda resisted the urge to word vomit all over Trey. Trey rubbed at Drew's back in silence. After patting his back once, Trey leaned back and sat quietly with Drew.

Drew stayed in that chair the whole night. Monsters came and went from the circle. Trey and Wynter went back and forth from the backyard to the house, leaving Drew to glare at the roaring fire pit. When his eyes grew tired of that, he rolled his head back and stared up at the oblivion. Blackness and speckled stars swallowed him the longer he stared.

His meditation was disrupted whenever his friends returned. Wynter always had a soda and snacks in tow. *"Have you ever eaten chips when you're sad? It's truly pathetic."* Drew's high had turned on him, making Panda even more un-bearable and cruel than usual.

Panda became louder, berating Drew at every turn. He reminded Drew of every shameful, awful thing that he'd ever done in his last seventeen years on earth. He repeated Sydney's hateful words and reminded Drew of the look on Miranda's face after they argued. Panda kept flashing the horrified look on his mom's face from earlier that afternoon through Drew's memory.

Drew barely had the strength to shut him up. He tried countering Panda with Trey's words. He deserved to be happy. For so long, Drew thought he was unworthy of happiness. All safety had been ripped away from him when his uncle abused him. His security was forever gone when he lost his dad. Love became unavailable as he built a wall between himself and his mom. Brick by brick, Drew had laid a foundation made of self-hatred, lies, drugs, doubt, anger, and fear. As his one chance to do good, he had put his sister on a pedestal.

Drew was so sick and tired of feeding Panda, his inner monster that he had given birth to from his own depression and anxiety, from the darkest part that he even refused to let his best friends see. It would be so easy to blame Panda for everything that had ever gone wrong in his life. But the truth was that Panda was just as lost as Drew. He was just as scared of criticism and abandonment.

"Let's go home," Wynter held her hand out to him.

Drew's bloodshot eyes looked up at her and then darted everywhere in confusion. The back yard was deserted now. The music inside was off.

"Is the party over?" Drew asked, dripping with sorrow.

"Yeah," Wynter nodded gently. "I'll walk you home."

Her raccoon was gone. Did Drew hallucinate all that? "*You know, I'm not sure. But I do know that the Miranda debacle was VERY real,*" Panda clarified. Drew just wanted to go home and hide beneath the covers and sink further into his despair. He was hoping to have a dreamless night. With a tight stomach and sweaty palms, he grabbed Wynter's hand. She held on as he eased his jelly legs up. They took their time crossing the lawn as Drew waited for feeling to return to his legs.

Trey was at the front door pushing people out of his house. Drew surveyed the house as Wynter dragged him along. It didn't look as bad as last year. The worst was the bathroom. The bathroom was always the worst. Panda shuddered thinking about it. Wynter felt him shake and wrapped an arm around his waist, thinking he was cold. Drew dropped his arm around her shoulders, pulling her in tighter.

"Thanks dude," Drew gave Trey a half-formed smile.

"Don't worry about it, man," Trey fist bumped Drew on their way out.

"We'll be here tomorrow to help you clean up," Wynter said as she passed by.

"Sleep in, please," Trey groaned. "Let's meet at

like…one."

Drew saluted him as Wynter walked him out the front door and headed them in the direction of his house. "You know," he rubbed her shoulder, "I'm the one who's supposed to be walking you home."

She smiled, "I doubt you can take three steps without tripping."

"You're probably right," Drew sighed heavily.

Panda filled their time with random thoughts. So long as he didn't say anything stupid, Drew was ok with taking a backseat. "Taxes are a yearly subscription to the country you're living in … If you're not supposed to take candy from strangers, then explain Halloween? … Your eraser dies because of your mistakes…" Wynter patiently listened, mumbling out agreements from time to time.

"Shit!" Drew's eyes widened in panic.

"What?" Wynter blinked at him in terror.

"My bag. I lost my bag. Omar is going to kill me."

"Nope," she patted him on the chest, resuming their walk. "You didn't bring it. You're done with Omar, remember?"

Patchy flashbacks came back to Drew as he forced his memory to return. "*Thank God!*" Drew and Panda were ready to crumble to the ground with exhaustion. Relieved of one less responsibility, Drew ran a tired hand down his face.

"What about my bike?"

"That, you did leave at Trey's," Wynter snickered. "You'll grab it tomorrow."

"Ok," Drew huffed.

They rounded the corner to his house. Dread seized in Drew's chest for a moment. "*Chill,*" Panda calmed. "*Liam's not there. And neither is Evie. Neither is Mom by the looks of it. She probably picked up a shift.*"

"Hey," Panda pressed. "I'm sorry about that bullshit last year. With Miranda, Porter, and Vitale. I'm sorry I didn't stand up for you."

Her brows bunched in surprise, "It's ok."

"No, it's not," Panda interrupted. "I should've done something. Kicked Vitale's ass. Not gone to prom with Miranda…"

She pushed off him a little and locked her fingers around his hand to keep him steady. The hand holding caused butterflies in his stomach. "I saw the fight between Trey and Sydney. You know it got ugly right?"

Drew nodded guiltily.

"Want to tell me about your fight with Miranda?"

Drew sighed heavily, "I just put my foot in my mouth with the one girl who liked me."

"She's not the only one," Wynter muttered under her breath. Louder, she said, "I'm here if you want to talk about it."

She didn't think Drew heard the first thing she said. But he did. And Panda so kindly put her words on repeat. "*She's not the only one.*" Drew stopped on the sidewalk. Wynter made it two steps ahead of him before their outstretched arms tugged her around to face him. Drew's eyes were glued on their hands still locked together. "*She's not the only one.*"

Wynter looked at him with confusion. "What?"

Drew licked his lips, his throat suddenly dry. "What did you mean by that?"

Her face twitched. She quickly threw on a dismissive smile. "What are you talking about?"

"What do you mean Miranda's not the only one?"

They stayed like that for a minute. Hands still clasped, a few feet between them, they anxiously stared at one another and waited for one of them to finally speak their truth.

Wynter eventually scoffed and dropped his hand, "Oh, come on, Drew."

He took a tentative step toward her, "Wynter?"

"What?" Her tone turned defensive. "You think Miranda is the only one who likes you?" Her eyes hardened when he didn't answer her. "I've been your friend for years, Drew. You never once thought of me?"

Stunned, Drew was paralyzed in place.

"*Is she really saying what we think she's saying?*" Panda was just as shocked.

"Of course, I have Wynter."

"*All the time,*" Drew nearly let Panda's thought slip out.

"I just thought…" Drew stammered.

"*What?*" Panda ranted. "*She's way too good for us! She's smarter than us. She's so beautiful it hurts to look at her sometimes. Wynter deserves someone better than us.*"

"I didn't think you liked me like that," Drew finally admitted.

Wynter blinked at him. She was stunned by his admission. For a moment, she wasn't sure of what to do next. Breathing evenly, she turned away from him and continued walking toward his house.

Drew came out of his stupor. He took four long strides and caught up with her. Reaching out, he grabbed her hand. She stopped but didn't turn toward him.

"Wyn," Drew whispered.

"Please don't!" She bunched her shoulders up to her ears.

"What does this mean for us?"

"It can't. I'm going to France next year."

Drew's heart sank as he took in her words. How long had she liked him? How many years did he waste when he could've been with her?

"I like YOU, Wynter," Drew confessed in a second of bravery.

Her back went straight. She turned to face him. Her face was furious but Panda noticed that she didn't let go of his hand. "And Miranda? You can't just go from girl to girl when things get hard, Drew."

His brows furrowed, "I know that."

Her face didn't relax.

"I'm sorry, Wynter. I didn't think I had a shot with you in a million years."

Drew had always liked Wynter. And things with Miranda were weird now. He didn't know where he stood with either girl. Would he even have tried to go out with Miranda if he thought he had a chance with Wynter? "*Probably not,*" Panda admitted.

"I really am sorry for not telling you sooner," Drew continued. "And you're right. I can't go from girl to girl."

He shrugged, not sure of what else to say. "All I know is that I like you. A lot," he chuckled to himself, certain he was blushing by now. "And it doesn't matter to me that you're going to France."

She stared at him for a moment, absorbing his words. Drew took a tentative step toward her. When she didn't recoil, he took another step. They were mere inches apart.

"Wyn," Drew let go of her hand briefly to hold her face. She closed her eyes, trying to reign her emotions in. "If you tell me to back off now, I will."

She opened her beautiful gray eyes. They had a glossy sheen to them. Her lips parted, but she couldn't get any words out. She sniffed. "I don't know what to do," she whispered, honestly.

Drew gave her a small smile, "I don't know either." Slowly, he brought his lips closer to hers. Centimeters from her mouth, he whispered, "Can I kiss you?"

She slowly nodded her head. He touched his lips to hers. Wynter and Drew seemed frozen for a moment, shocked that they were kissing each other, in awe of it all. Drew breathed her in. She smelt faintly of weed and cocoa butter. And something else. Something so rich and earthly. Something that was just her.

She reached her arms around his neck, trapping him in place. He brought her closer to his chest and gripped her tightly. Hungry gasps passed between them as they kissed with more urgency. Panda ran laps around them with sparklers in hand, cheering loudly. Her hands moved down to his waist, pulling him closer. He held onto her face. That soft, round face that could be scrunched up with anger at him one minute and dazzling with a bright smile the next. Drew's heart felt like it might explode. All his worries and self-doubt had completely vanished in this moment.

And then he felt Wynter's hands tug at his shirt as it brushed against his skin.

The scars on his hips hummed in response.

Drew pulled back with a gasp. "*What happened?*" Panda whined. "*Why did you stop?*" Drew took a step back, dazed. He desperately heaved for air.

Panting, Wynter looked at him with wide eyes. "What's wrong?"

Drew shook his head side to side, "I don't think I can, uh..." he fixed his shirt, self-conscious of the three scars on his hip. "*Shit,*" Panda contemplated. "*I didn't think anyone would ever like us. Or would want to touch and see our skin. I'm sorry Drew...*" Even with Panda's apology, Drew's discomfort grew as he thought about his other scars on his legs.

Her eyes flashed to his waist. She realized what she'd done. "Drew..." she took a tentative step forward. "You know I don't judge you, right?" He took another step back. She paused. "I think you're beautiful."

He stared at her with disbelief. How could she not judge him? He'd marred his flesh! All in a moment of weakness, when he was unable to regulate his emotions. He thought cutting himself would solve his problems. Flaws, mistakes, and shame forever haunted his body. How could he possibly be beautiful?

"I'm sorry, Wyn. I don't think I can do this." Drew brushed past her and hurriedly shoved his keys in the lock of his front door.

"Drew let's talk about this. Please!" Wynter's words rushed out.

"I'll see you tomorrow. I'm sorry."

CHAPTER TWENTY-ONE

"Drew," a gentle breeze caressed his ear, followed by an annoying, gentle poke to his face. "Drew," he heard again.

He hummed in answer and then groaned like an irritated bear stirred too soon out of hibernation. Not ready to open his eyes. Panda rolled off him, allowing him to shift his head. "Mom said it's time to get up. She's making us grilled cheeses," Evie purred with excitement.

"Eves?" Drew attempted to open an eye. Heavy crust kept both eyes sealed. "What time is it?"

"I don't know." She thought about it for a minute, "Lunch time?"

"Hey," he rolled on his side and managed to peel an eye open. "How was the sleepover?"

"It was awesome!" Evie answered too loudly.

"Charlotte has this cute dog named Beverly…"

Drew let her carry on for a moment as he sat up and rubbed at his eyes. The last thing he wanted to do today was clean Trey's house. But if he didn't, Trey would never throw another party in the history of high school again. Forgetting he was shirtless, he let his sheet fall to his waist, accidentally exposing the three rigid scars to Evie. She stopped talking and her attention drifted down. More alert, he covered himself quickly. She reached a small hand over to him and tugged the sheet back down so she could get a good look at them.

Drew stared at her wildly as vulnerability clawed at him. He regretted cutting his body up. He regretted how it distanced him from intimacy, and how it kept him from wearing what he wanted. It was a constant lie to himself and others. Another mark of weakness that he couldn't get his shit together.

Her small pudgy fingers gently stroked the puffy, discolored skin. Her face was soft, neutral. "Did he do this to you?" Her tone was light, but felt like an abrasion with its gentleness.

Drew's heart picked up its pace. "What are you talking

about, Eves?"

She craned her head over to Panda who was perfectly still, staring up at the ceiling, wishing the bed would swallow him. "Him!" Evie pointed right at Panda. Panda jolted upright.

"You can see him?"

"*You can see me?*"

Drew and Panda spoke over each other.

She shrugged nonchalantly. "Sometimes."

Drew and Panda looked at each other in disbelief. Each was ready to blame the other for letting the secret out.

"He's really loud and kind of mean to people. Like Uncle Liam. Is Uncle Liam not here anymore because of him?"

Drew sighed. He was so not ready for this conversation. Especially not after just waking up. And not ever with his little sister. Panda shrank back against the wall in cowardice. "No," Drew slightly shook his head, "Uncle Liam was mean to him first."

"Is that why he's mean? Why he hurts you?" She looked back over to Panda. Empathy clouded her gaze.

"Yeah," Drew nodded. "He's not mean to you. Is he?"

She shook her head. "No, he's nice to me."

"Evie," Drew swung his legs to the edge of the bed

revealing more of his scars. Panda would've smacked Drew upside the head if Evie wasn't watching him like a hawk. In exasperation, Drew covered himself quickly with the blanket. She didn't act any differently seeing he had more scars. "How can you see him?"

"I have one too."

"One what?" Drew cocked his head. Panda leaned forward, intrigued.

"My teacher, Mrs. Spencer, calls him imaginary. But he's real, not imaginary. And if you have one, then Mr. Sprinkles has to be real. He's my friend."

"*Mr. Sprinkles?*" Panda asked. "*Why does that name sound familiar?*"

Evie turned to Panda with approval. "He's a unicorn."

"Mr. Sprinkles?" Drew asked with skepticism. Evie nodded in confirmation. He shook his head. "Why can't I see him?"

She just shrugged in answer.

"Can he see Panda?"

"Sometimes."

"*Does he talk about us?*" Panda leaned in closer to her, nervous that he could be seen and judged by an invisible entity.

"Sometimes," Evie answered honestly.

"*What does Mr. Sprinkles say about us?*" Panda bit at a nail.

Evie put her hand on his knee. This calmed Panda instantly. "He's sad to see you mad all the time. He just wants to give you a hug. Mom says hugs make everything better."

Drew clenched his jaw, fighting back tears as his heart swelled. "Is Mr. Sprinkles around all the time?" he asked. Drew thought about how Panda had been with him every day for the last year. Before that it was just during heightened moments of stress.

Evie turned back to Drew, shaking her head. "No. He's just around whenever I'm sad. Or when I need someone to play with. His favorite thing to play is tea-time," she smiled proudly.

Drew stared at her with astonishment, as if he were seeing his sister for the first time.

"*She needs Mr. Sprinkles when she's sad,*" Panda mused.

Drew swallowed thickly, wondering how often she was sad. "What does Mr. Sprinkles think of Mom? Of Uncle Liam?"

She pushed her lips to the side in thought. "We miss Mom. She seems sad all the time. I wish Dad was here. He always made her happy," Evie smiled in remembrance.

Drew's eyes coated as he remembered how his mom used to laugh when his dad was around. "And Uncle Liam?"

"Mr. Sprinkles likes that he looks like Dad. He gets confused and sad when I tell him Dad's gone." Her shoulders slumped as she shared her imaginary friend's feelings.

"I miss Dad too," Drew took a deep breath.

Evie nodded in agreement.

"Do you miss Uncle Liam?" Drew hesitated to ask.

She moved her lips from side to side in thought and finally raised her shoulders in a shrug.

Drew nodded. It was a complicated question for a seven year old. His nose flared and silence fell around them as he took in her words. He resisted the inclination to cry. Drew had never felt so seen in all his life. He couldn't believe that Evie could see all of him, even the part of himself that he worked so hard to keep hidden from everyone. Evie saw it all. And she didn't treat him any differently. Panda was already a blubbering mess beside him.

"What's your name?" Evie cocked her head at him.

"*My name?*" Panda wiped an arm across his snotty nose.

Drew just shrugged, "I call him Panda."

"I know WHAT he is," Evie sassed. She put her hands on

her hips, "He needs a name."

"He does?" Drew raised a brow.

"Mrs. Spencer says everyone needs a name." She looked at Panda, and then waited with an air of tranquility on her face.

Panda looked to Drew, pleading for help.

Drew just looked at him. He was trying to accept him too.

"*Can I be…Stevie?*" Panda looked back at Evie.

She grinned broadly. "It's perfect!"

"Guys!" Celeste's voice echoed down the stairs. "Time to eat!"

Still covering himself with the blanket, Drew reached over to grab his black pants off the floor. But Evie was faster and ran over and stepped on them. Drew nearly punched himself in the face from losing grip.

"Hey!"

"It's nice today. I think you should wear shorts."

Panda struggled to retort.

"Eves," Drew started, "you're the only one who knows."

"About Stevie?"

"No," Drew groaned, "well yes. But I'm talking about my scars."

Evie shrugged. "It's just you."

Stumped, he tried to swallow the lump in his throat. "Go help Mom and Mr. Sprinkles." He poked at her side. Her foot lifted off his pants in a fit of giggles. Drew quickly grabbed them and she ran upstairs for refuge.

Drew stared at his pants for a moment.

"*Holy shit*," Pand—Stevie gasped. "*Man, that's going to take some getting used to.*"

"Which part? The fact that my little sister can see you sometimes, or that I have to call you Stevie now?"

Stevie shrugged, "*Both.*"

Drew found a clean, but wrinkly, white crew neck to wear. He quickly brushed his teeth, washed his face, and rolled some deodorant on. He stared at his clothing options on the bed. He had a pair of black cargo shorts he'd never worn that his mom bought two summers ago, or his normal black pants.

"*How brave are we feeling today?*" Stevie patted Drew on the back.

"Drew!" Evie snickered to herself when he came into view from the top of the stairs.

Celeste's smile slipped as her eyes drifted down Drew's legs. She stared at him widely, placing a hand over her mouth to conceal her trembling lip.

He hurried over to the table, uncomfortable under her observation. He briskly bit into his grilled cheese sandwich and grabbed a handful of grapes with his free hand before Evie ate them all. Avoiding his mom's weepy look, he reached down and scratched at his bare calf self-consciously.

Drew forced the rest of the congealed sandwich down his throat. "Thanks for lunch, Mom."

She blinked a few times and cleared her throat. "You're welcome. Any plans today?"

Drew looked at the clock. "I'm going to Trey's for a bit. In like half an hour?"

"Are you working today, Mom?" Evie kicked her legs under the table.

"I've got a night shift. Last one on rotation. I've…" Celeste cleared her throat, "…my schedule has been moved around."

"Meaning?" Stevie asked around a mouthful of grapes.

"Starting next Monday, I'm working seven to four. And maybe every other Saturday."

Evie cocked her head to the side as she tried to put it together.

"So," Drew clarified, "you'll be home more?"

Celeste's lips curled inward. "Yeah," she said with a thoughtful nod.

"That's awesome, Mom." Drew gave her a half-formed smile. It was the best he could do. *"One brave thing at a time,"* Stevie reassured him.

"And I'm going to see if another mom in Evie's class can help me with picking her up and dropping her off," Celeste continued.

Evie pouted, "Does that mean Drew won't take me anymore? Or pick me up?"

Celeste leaned in close to her, "We'll see."

"I don't mind doing it," Drew spoke up. He wasn't exactly ready to relinquish the time spent with his little sister.

"I know you've been ditching," Celeste straightened. Drew waited for her eyes to start burning with anger. But it didn't come.

"I still passed," Drew shrugged.

Celeste sighed. "I understand why you took her to school so Liam wouldn't have to. Let's see what your schedule is like. I don't want you skipping anymore." Her tone was final. Not angry like Drew had expected it, but respectful. At least she was open to Drew taking his little sister if his schedule allowed it.

Drew nodded. He made a mental note to go to the school tomorrow and request that he have seventh period off next year. He was willing to compromise with his mom. If he couldn't take Evie in the morning, then he was going to at least pick her up in the afternoon!

His eyes drifted toward the TV in the living room. His mom didn't usually have it on while they ate. Evie must've been watching cartoons while Celeste got lunch together. The local news flashed across the screen with the sound muted. Drew could read the headline perfectly.

"Showdown Between Rival Drug Gangs: One Dead and One in Critical Condition…"

Drew stared at the TV. His heart felt like it stopped beating. He held his breath and squinted, trying to read the delayed subtitles as the news reporters explained what happened.

"…yesterday afternoon. Wallace Rhames is currently being detained by the police at the hospital. He is still in critical condition."

"Everything ok, Drew?" His mom asked softly. Her eyes darted between her son and the TV. His face was sunken. He blinked slowly in astonishment.

"If Wallace is the one in critical condition…" Stevie started putting the pieces together. Drew kept watching. Interviews with neighbors came on next.

"Do you know something about that?" Celeste asked with a hitch in her voice, suddenly worried that her son had been involved in the shootout yesterday.

"Well, you were," Stevie shrugged in shame. But he wasn't about tell his mom that.

"No, but I knew them," Drew answered semi-honestly. "Last year, ya know?"

Celeste nodded in understanding. Together, they eyed the TV. Drew and Stevie held their breath until the news reel repeated itself. "Local residents of the View Apartments were disturbed yesterday afternoon as two rival drug gangs opened fire on each other. The resident, Omar Russell, was killed during the altercation. Wallace Rhames has been arrested by police and is being treated for critical injuries. Other associates at the scene have also been detained. Police have not reported any other injured individuals…"

Drew nearly choked on a grape. Omar was gone.

"Deceased, departed, perished, dead as a door nail, pushing up daisies!" Stevie gasped in shock.

He was well and truly gone. Drew looked back to his

mom. She had a worry line between her brows. Without thinking about it, he smiled at her. His mom was safe. Evie was safe. Only Omar knew where Drew lived. And without him, "*it means we really are out,*" Stevie chuckled quietly in disbelief.

A knock at the door echoed into the room. All three of them exchanged confused looks. "It might be Trey or Wynter," Drew cleared his throat and stood up, shoving a couple more grapes in his mouth. Stevie's heart thundered at the thought of Wynter. "*Oh My God! I haven't even begun about WYNTER!*"

Drew crossed the room, calming Stevie down at the prospect of seeing his best friend. Drew and Stevie dared a quick glance to the side of the room. Maybe it was that his mom dusted, or maybe it was the way the early afternoon sunlight from the window bounced off the frame, but his father's shrine looked less haunted. Serene even. "*Hey Dad,*" Stevie waved to the photo. A smile tugged at the corner of Drew's mouth. Drew opened the door and his stomach dropped what felt like twenty feet.

"Hey," Miranda waved shyly. "Sorry to just…" she snorted apprehensively, "…show up at your house like this."

"It's ok," Drew shooed her back some as he stepped

outside, closing the door behind him.

He was surprised she remembered where he lived. It was weeks ago when her mom dropped them off when he and Miranda had first worked on their project. She didn't come into his house. She had waited in the car with Maddy, watching as their moms stood in the yard and talked for like ten minutes. And that was that. And now here she was, the last person Drew wanted to be face-to-face with right now.

Drew rubbed the building sweat on his palms onto his shorts. "Listen, about last night. I'm really sorry for blowing up at you like that. I was really high."

She blinked at him, surprised by his open admission.

"Not that that's an excuse. But it was…" Drew suddenly ran dry with his explanation. Scratching the back of his neck, he continued, "…really dumb. I could've handled it better."

She pushed her lips to the side. "Thank you," she bobbed her head slightly. "I actually came over to apologize too." When Drew and Stevie didn't say anything, she continued, "You were right. I should've stood up against Sydney. Stood up FOR Wynter. I was too scared and ended up hurting someone."

"Oh," Drew leaned back a bit. "Thanks."

"Wynter seems pretty cool," Miranda shrugged.

"Yeah," Drew cleared his throat, "she is. You know she's going to France next year?" The confused twist of Miranda's face told Drew that she didn't know. "Maybe you could spend some time with her over the summer before she leaves."

Her chocolate curls fell over her shoulders as she shook her head. "I don't think she likes me."

"You should give each other a chance."

She pressed her lips together, not really wanting to talk about another girl right now. As the silence stretched between them, the air grew thick with awkwardness. "So…" Miranda tried.

"So?"

"Where does this leave us?" She squinted a little at him from the bright sun in her eyes. "Because I've got to say, Drew, I didn't really appreciate you blowing up on me like that."

"Um…" Drew pressed his lips together, trying to contain Stevie. *"We can't go out with her now that we know how WYNTER feels! Right? Oh, maybe we could keep them both. Wyn's leaving in like two months! No. No. That'd be a dick move. Holy shit…do we have two girls interested in us AT THE SAME TIME?! DUDE! This is never going to happen again. But you really should decide. It's not fair to drag someone along.*" Drew sighed heavily, "Miranda…"

He could feel Miranda's optimism deplete. Her forced smile slipped as reality slowly sank in. Her eyes cast downward but immediately came back to his face as she fought the urge to let her face falter.

Drew glanced down, realizing that he'd left the house in a pair of shorts. He was thankful in that moment that his scars were mostly on the back of his legs. There was one jagged scar on the side. But still, he'd gone outside in shorts! For the first time in four years, he felt what it was like to have the wind tickle his leg hair. "*Do you think she would find us ugly if she knew the truth?*" Stevie echoed Drew's insecurity.

His heart sank as he saw the look on Miranda's face. Drew recognized it from when his classmates found out his dad died. He had seen it from his friends a few times, and always from his mom. Liam faked it. But never Evie, thank God. It was pity. How he hated that look. The yearn to hug him. Comfort him. "*Fix us.*"

Drew cleared his throat loudly. Their eyes met again. "I don't think I want to be with you, Miranda."

Her body flinched. He watched as her heart literally shattered on the porch in front of his feet.

"I'm sorry, but I'm just not in a good place right now," Drew hurriedly said hoping to salvage a few pieces of her heart. But it was too late. He'd broken it. And if he was being one hundred percent honest, he'd broken a small piece of his heart too. "You deserve better than me right now."

"Yeah, uh…" Miranda nodded. She cared about Drew, a lot. But she wasn't going to argue with someone who didn't want to be with her.

When Miranda didn't finish her sentence, Drew instinctively took a step back and rambled on, "I'm sorry, Miranda. You're a great girl. And I really hope we can be friends. Because you're great…"

Rolling his eyes, Stevie grumbled, "*You said that already.*"

"…but I need some time to myself right now," Drew finished.

Miranda's nose flared. Those bright brown eyes that gave Drew butterflies barely a day ago grew hard. She forced a tight-lipped smile. Her eyes watered. She blinked furiously, trying to dispel the oncoming tears. She took a step back and then inhaled sharply, "Uh, Evie is always welcome to hang out with Maddison. And maybe we can hang out again."

"Yeah, maybe. I appreciate that."

She hummed her answer, nodded, and took a few more

steps backward. "I'm going to head out."

Drew flicked his hand up halfway to his waist in an attempted wave. She turned viciously on her heel. Drew commended Miranda for keeping her head high. But he saw the slight tremor in her shoulders. He watched her for a moment as her pace quickened down the sidewalk.

"*Harsh but good job,*" Stevie nodded.

"Sheesh," Drew sighed heavily, rubbing at his face, "that was awful." Stevie patted his back as they turned toward the door.

"*Does that mean we can be with Wynter now?*" Stevie asked earnestly.

Drew sighed, unsure. "We're still a screwed-up mess right now. Neither Miranda nor Wynter deserve that. I wasn't lying, dude, we need some time for ourselves."

For once, Stevie didn't argue back. He just nodded and patted Drew's his back as they went inside. Drew caught Celeste and Evie awkwardly sitting on the couch, clearly busted for spying on him through the window. He assumed Evie had told their mom all about Miranda by now.

"Any questions?" Drew asked as if he were a TV host. He crossed his arms in mock annoyance.

"You ok?" his mom climbed off the couch.

Drew waved her off, "I'll be fine." He huffed slightly, and gestured to Evie, "She said you can still hang out with Maddison if you want."

"Oh good," Evie sighed, relieved.

Before Drew could close the door, Trey's car pulled up. The loud music faded as the tires rolled to a stop. Trey's eyes were concealed by dark sunglasses and he looked like he was trying to massage away a headache. Wynter was in the front passenger seat, looking fresh with a bright smile.

She hung out the window and shouted, "Trey needs tacos before we get started!"

Drew held up his index finger and patted down his pockets. Wallet, check. Keys, check. Phone, check. He turned back to his mom and Evie. "Alright," he said, holding his arms out. Evie crashed into him. "I'll be back later."

"Back for dinner?" Celeste stepped closer, putting a hand on his shoulder.

Drew smirked and nodded his head, "Sure." He jogged outside, not bothering to change his clothes.

Drew and Stevie climbed in the back seat. Celeste and Evie waved goodbye as the loud music resumed and Trey sped away toward his greasy food respite. Wynter carried on about all the gossip she collected from last night. Trey occasionally grunted. Drew leaned back in his seat, letting the wind hit his face.

"You good?" Wynter half turned to him. Big silver eyes matched her smile.

"Yeah," Drew felt his eyes squint slightly as the corners of his mouth spread.

Stevie stuck his head out of the window like a dog just happy to be there. The wind tickled through his fur. Drew noticed how calm his heartbeat was as he stared out the window and watched the vibrant, green trees pass by. The bright blue sky seemed endless. Large puffy clouds formed random shapes. Children played in their front yards, their laughter drifting in and out of the car. People walked their eager dogs. Music from other cars competed for attention. Drew was comforted by Trey's deep laugh and the sweet sound of Wynter's voice.

Today was a nice day.

Acknowledgements

I never thought I'd get to the point that I'd be making an acknowledgement page. I could not have done it without all the help and support of those nearest and dearest to me. Thank you all.

To you, my readers: Thank you for taking a chance on me and this book. Parts of myself are in this book. If you struggle with your own inner voice, I hope we are connected now and you're not alone in your struggles.

To my editor, Jen: I have grown immensely as a writer thanks to your help editing this book. Nothing can ever prepare you to be critique like this, but you were always so kind, patient, and communicative with me. I really enjoyed the process and working with you. I hope we can work on future projects together. Thank you for everything!

To my parents (Lisa, Dean, Jeff and Amy): I would not be who I am without each of you. Each helping me through different parts in my life. Though our family was never perfect, I'm grateful to have you as my parents.

To my brother, Bishop (Robin, Ulv): We have shared many relationships over our years. Sibling, protector, friend, roommate, and collaborator. Regardless of which hat we're wearing that day, know that I will always love you. And thank you for bringing Drew and Panda to life!

To my friend, Annie (Anna-Fred, my oldest friend): I know I would've lost my mind a long time ago if it weren't for your unconditional love, friendship, and support. Thanks for always sharing space with me, dude!

To my friend, Naomi (Queen, Darling): I am so thankful we were both brave enough to become friends. Thank you for always being in my corner. And I cannot believe my dumb luck of you having an editor as an aunt! I am forever grateful for the introduction.

To my beta reader, Desbie (Doobs, Desbie Marie): I can never thank you enough for being my beta reader. Helping my dream come true and making sure the book was ready for the rest of the world. Despite this growth in our friendship, I will still start our conversations with an awkward pause before I begin talking.

To my love, Armando: You see all of me. Giving me the confidence to keep going. Always in my corner and being my loudest cheerleader. And I am thankful each day you are in my life. I love you.

About the Author

Monique Russ loves creating stories with diverse characters. Characters that are perfectly imperfect. She lives in the Rocky Mountains close to family and friends and is a proud cat stepmom. Connect with her here!

TikTok: @moniqueruss_author

Goodreads: goodreads.com/moniqueruss_author

Website: moniqueruss.com